The
Secret
School

ALSO BY AVI:

Bright Shadow

Don't You Know There's a War On?

Ereth's Birthday

The Fighting Ground

Nothing But the Truth: A Documentary Novel

Poppy

Poppy and Rye

Ragweed

Romeo and Juliet—Together (and Alive!) at Last

S.O.R. Losers

Tom, Babette & Simon: Three Tales of Transformation

The True Confessions of Charlotte Doyle

Who Stole the Wizard of Oz?

"Who Was That Masked Man, Anyway?"

The Secret School

AVI

HARCOURT, INC.
San Diego   New York   London

A shorter version of this novel was published in newspapers
throughout the country as part of the Breakfast Serials program.

www.harcourt.com

Library of Congress Cataloging-in-Publication Data
Avi, 1937–
The secret school/Avi.
p.   cm.
Summary: In 1925, fourteen-year-old Ida Bidson secretly takes
over as the teacher when the one-room schoolhouse in her remote
Colorado area closes unexpectedly.   [1. Teachers—Fiction.
2. One-room schools—Fiction.   3. Schools—Fiction.
4. Sex role—Fiction.   5. Colorado—Fiction.]   I. Title.
PZ7.A953Se   2001
[Fic]—dc21   2001000629
ISBN 0-15-216375-1

Text set in Bembo
Designed by Cathy Riggs

First edition
A C E G H F D B

Printed in the United States of America

For my friends and colleagues
at the Eugene Field Library

One

❦

ON A COOL MONDAY morning in early
April 1925, Ida Bidson, aged fourteen, carefully
guided her family's battered Model T Ford along a
narrow, twisting dirt road in Elk Valley, Colorado.

"Brake and clutch!" she shouted.

Ida, only four-feet-eleven and unable to reach
the floor of the car, knelt on the torn seat and
gripped the steering wheel tightly. Her seven-year-
old brother, Felix, hunched on the floor before her
and used his hands to push the brake and clutch
pedals down.

As Ida adjusted the throttle lever, the battered

car, hiccuping like a damp firecracker, swung into a sharp turn. "Less brake!" Ida called.

"Where we at?" Felix called up as he leaned onto the right pedal.

"It's 'Where are we?'" his older sister corrected.

"You're not my teacher! Just tell me!"

"We're close. Less brake!"

The car bumped along, causing the old tin syrup can filled with their lunch to bounce on the seat beside Ida. Behind them, dust twirled out like an unraveling rope, momentarily hiding the high ring of snowcapped mountains that surrounded the valley.

As the car churned up a hill—with enough backfiring to suggest a small war had erupted—Ida caught sight of Tom Kohl and his younger sister, Mary, riding bareback on their mule, Ruckus. Best friends, Ida and Tom were forever talking about all kinds of things: their plans, their friends, their families, what was going on in the valley.

Seeing him, Ida grinned, reached over the door—the car had no windows—and squeezed the horn bulb attached to the outside of the car. *Honnnk! Honnnk!*

At the loud gooselike sound, Ruckus gave a little buck. Though startled, Tom skillfully reined the mule to the side of the road, then turned around and pushed his floppy flaxen hair out of his eyes. Seeing Ida's slow-moving car, he smiled and yelled, "Get yourself a mule!"

"Join the twentieth century!" she shouted back.

"Who's there?" Felix called from the floor.

"Tom and Mary. Now pay attention. We're almost there. Brake easy!"

The car finally rounded the last bend, bringing Elk Valley's schoolhouse into view. The building stood in the middle of its own small north-south valley, through which the dirt road ran. To the east low hills gave way to higher ground, woods, and mountains. West it was much the same. Squat and square, the school building had a pitched roof and a small bell steeple at the south end. The painted but peeling white clapboard walls had three windows on each side. Beyond the school stood two privies, one for boys and one for girls. To the south was a small shallow pond. In front of the school stood a flagpole not far from a water pump as well as a lopsided teeter-totter.

"Clutch to neutral and brake!" Ida shouted as she aimed the car toward its regular parking place, only to realize that another car—one she didn't recognize—was already there.

"Hold on!" Ida screamed. With all her strength, she turned the wheel hard about, then yelled, "Brake!" as she grabbed the hand lever and pulled back.

Barely avoiding a crash, the old Ford came to a lurching halt next to the other car. Its motor gave one more enormous backfire, sputtered, chuffed twice, then died with a shuddering sigh.

"We're here," Ida announced. Her heart was pounding.

"What happened?" Felix asked.

"Another car was parked in our spot. I almost hit it."

"Whose car?"

"Don't know."

Ida tightened the brake, then untied the rope that held the side door shut. With a squeak it swung open. "Out you go!" she called.

Felix, crawling headfirst, slipped down to the ground.

"I hate this," he complained as he stretched his arms and legs.

"Beats walking five miles both ways," Ida said as she got out and looked toward the school. She brushed the dust from her braided brown hair and checked to see if her blue ribbons were still tied tightly. Then she smoothed down her gingham dress. Of all the dresses her mother had made for her, this was her favorite.

Herbert Bixler, Charley and Susie Spool, and Natasha Golobin were seated on the school's front porch. As Ida and Felix approached, they all looked up.

"Looky here!" Herbert shouted gleefully. "I'm back!"

"And he's already tried to tie my shoelaces together," Susie complained.

Herbert lifted one of his bare feet and wiggled his toes. "Guess I don't know much about how shoes work," he said.

Ida ignored him. "Whose car is that?" she asked.

Natasha, who was a year younger than Ida, replied, "Mr. Jordan's."

Mr. Jordan was the owner-operator of Wally's Mighty Fine Emporium, Elk Valley's feed and grocery store. He was also head of the school board.

"Guess he can park anywhere he wants," Ida acknowledged. "How come he's here?"

Herbert shrugged. "Dunno."

"Is Miss Fletcher here?" Felix asked.

"Inside," Charley assured them. Charley and

Susie, who lived just over the hill, were always the first to get to school.

"What's Mr. Jordan's car doing here?" Tom called as he slid off Ruckus, then helped his sister down. "He come for inspection?" As always, Tom tied the mule to the rear bumper of the Bidsons' car with enough rope to allow for grazing.

"No one knows," Ida replied.

Just then the schoolhouse door opened and Miss Fletcher appeared. A slight, middle-aged woman with dark hair piled atop her head, she was dressed in a simple blue cotton dress.

"Children," she said, "come in quickly, please. There's grave news to share."

The children exchanged puzzled looks.

"What's that supposed to mean?" Herbert muttered as soon as Miss Fletcher went back in.

"Shhh!" Ida hissed at him. "Don't sass!"

Felix said, "She didn't even say her regular 'Good morning.'"

Natasha added, "Wasn't even smiling."

"Guess we better get ourselves in and see," Tom said, always the logical one.

Without another word, the children climbed up the porch stairs and filed inside.

The school had but one room. Built entirely of

wood from the nearby Columbine lumber mill, the building was twenty years old. Most of the room was filled with ancient low benches and long student desks etched with countless initials. The desks were older than the school building. To the right of the front door was the boys' wardrobe. On the other side was the girls'. Miss Fletcher's desk stood on the left, close to a small wall-mounted blackboard, which at the moment was perfectly clean.

An aspen switch—for discipline—hung alongside the board. Next to that was the school's library, a small bookcase containing some fifteen tattered books plus a few old magazines.

A round, iron wood-burning stove stood to the right, opposite the teacher's desk. Kerosene lamps were fastened on each wall along with pictures of George Washington and Abraham Lincoln, and a chart of the Palmer script alphabet. There were also pull-down maps of Colorado, the United States, and the rest of the world.

As Miss Fletcher stood by the door, the eight students put away their lunch pails and their coats, then took their regular seats at their desks.

Felix and Mary, who were first and second graders, sat up front. Ida and Tom, the only eighth graders, took their places in the back row. Ida, being short, fit easily. Tom, tall and skinny, had to stretch out to get his knees to fit. The other four children—fourth through seventh graders—were scattered about on the other benches.

Mr. Jordan was standing in a corner going through Miss Fletcher's school account book. He was a portly, red-faced man, wearing overalls and a blue shirt. He had left his straw hat on the teacher's desk, something the children would never be allowed to do.

Ida, using a trick she had mastered long ago, faced front but whispered to Tom without moving her lips. "Why do you think he's here?"

"Don't know," Tom replied in the same stealthy fashion. "My old man says he's as miserly as a sleeping marmot."

Ida dipped her head to hide her grin.

Miss Fletcher stood before her desk, hands clasped, an unconvincing smile on her face.

"Good morning, children," the teacher began in her soft voice. "I'm so very glad the whole school's in attendance. Even you, Herbert Bixler."

Herbert roused himself from his slouch. "Miss Fletcher, it's my dad. He's always needing me to work. Weren't for him, I'd be sitting here every day being a high-marks scholar."

"Well, yes, we shan't discuss that now," Miss Fletcher replied. Composing herself, she looked down, then up at the class.

"Children," she began, "as I'm sure most of you know, this is Mr. Jordan, head of our local school board. Please greet him politely."

"Good-morning-Mister-Jordan," the children chorused.

"This morning," Miss Fletcher went on, "I'm afraid I must share painful news with you."

The children sat up stiffly.

"Last Friday," she continued, "I received a telegram telling me that my mother, back east in Iowa, has become very ill."

"Oh no!" Felix said loudly.

"Naturally," Mr. Jordan cut in, "Miss Fletcher needs to be there. And since there's only a month and a half till term ends, the school board won't be looking for a replacement. As soon as she departs..." He turned to the teacher. "When's that going to be, Miss Fletcher?"

"I'll be taking the Wednesday train," she replied.

"After which," Mr. Jordan continued, "school

will be closed. And it won't commence till the fall term, assuming, of course, we can hire us up a new teacher."

Ida and Tom exchanged looks of shock.

Mr. Jordan went on. "This means you can have one long summer vacation. I'm sure," he chortled, "that despite our sorrow at losing Miss Fletcher, that'll cheer you up."

Tom raised a hand.

"Yes, Tom?" Miss Fletcher said.

"I'm awful sorry for your trouble, Miss Fletcher. I truly am. But does that mean Ida and I won't be taking our exit exams?"

Miss Fletcher started to speak but held back. Instead she looked to Mr. Jordan for the answer.

"Exit exams? Well...," he said after a moment's thought, "we could hardly get us a new teacher on such short notice. So, yes, I guess your exams will have to wait till next year."

Ida lifted her hand.

"Yes, Ida?" Miss Fletcher said.

"Mr. Jordan," Ida said, "if Tom and I don't pass our exams *this* term, we can't go on to the high school in Steamboat Springs come fall."

Miss Fletcher turned to Mr. Jordan. "I'm afraid

that what Ida is saying is correct," she said. "They can't move on without those tests."

"Now, Ida Bidson," Mr. Jordan answered, "as an adult, it's my bounden duty to inform you—as I'm certain your parents do every day—that life teaches us many a hard lesson beyond school. No doubt this...exam business will be inconvenient.

"But I'd suggest you think a little less of yourself and a little more on Miss Fletcher and her ailing mother. Besides, I'm not so sure a girl needs a high school education. Any more questions?" Mr. Jordan asked, looking around the room.

Humiliated, Ida shrank down.

No one dared say anything else.

After shaking hands with Miss Fletcher, Mr. Jordan left.

The children gazed at Miss Fletcher.

"Miss Fletcher...," Ida said, on the verge of tears.

"Yes, Ida?"

"I...I am grieved for you and your mother. But you know how much I want to be a teacher. I *have* to graduate this year. This is my one chance. What am I supposed to do?"

Miss Fletcher sighed. "Ida," she said, "I want

you to know I begged Mr. Jordan not to close down the school. As for your exam and graduation—and Tom's—I can't rightly say what will happen. I . . . I will be gone. I am so sorry."

Silence filled the room.

"In the meanwhile," Miss Fletcher said softly, "we had best skip our morning song and get on with today's lessons." Quickly, she gave out the assignments.

The other children pulled out books and papers and began to work. Ida, sitting in numb silence, stared before her. All she was aware of was an enormous pain in her chest.

Two

DURING MIDMORNING recess Ida and Tom sat together against the west side of the school building. Tom, eyes closed, tilted his face up toward the sun. Ida pensively braided bits of grass.

"Tom," Ida said sadly, "I won't ever get to be a teacher without going to high school." She flung away the grass. "Course, my folks probably wouldn't have had the money for me to board in town, anyway. So I guess it doesn't really matter."

"Sure it does," Tom said.

"Well, then, it doesn't matter that it matters," Ida said, snatching up another blade of grass and twisting it tightly around a finger. "You have any idea how much Miss Fletcher earns?" she said after a while.

"Nope," Tom said.

"Forty dollars each month, that's what."

"Banana oil!" Tom cried. "How'd you know?"

"Start of the year, I saw her contract on her desk."

"Sneak-peek!"

"Suppose I was. But, if I had all that money…"

"What would you do?"

"Teach in a big city. Denver, maybe. Have books. My own car. A new one. Travel round the whole world."

"Come on, you're no flapper. Nice girls don't do that."

"Then, I'm not nice," Ida snapped. "And what about your electricity and radio? Not likely you'll do much of that 'less you get yourself some high school learning."

"I know," Tom agreed. He gazed out at the mountains that ringed Elk Valley. Ida followed his look. At the moment the surrounding peaks felt like a cage.

Tom said, "I suppose I can learn some of what I need from a correspondence course. Saw an ad for one in a copy of *Popular Mechanics*."

"Remember how Miss Fletcher told us weeks ago the exams were hard?" Ida said. "I'd already started studying."

"Well, then, guess it's time for a girl to have herself some fun."

Ida jumped up, hands on hips. "Tom Kohl," she yelled, braids almost flying off her head with fury, "you're such a sponge cake!" She stormed away.

"For crying out loud, Ida!" Tom called after her. "I was just kidding!"

Ida refused to turn about. She marched past the little kids playing on the teeter-totter.

Just up and down, she thought. *Going nowhere. Suppose if I'm not going to graduate, I won't be going anywhere, either.*

Reaching the other side of the school yard, Ida pumped up some cold water. As she drank from the tin cup that hung there from a string, Miss Fletcher opened the schoolhouse door.

"Ida, please come in!" she called. "I'd like to talk to you."

Not at all sure she wanted to talk, Ida went into the schoolhouse and sat down on the front-row bench.

Miss Fletcher took her place behind the desk.

For a moment they sat in silence.

"I want you to know how sorry I am," Miss Fletcher finally said. "I know how much you were set on going to high school."

"It's not your fault," Ida conceded. "Anyway, maybe your mother will get better soon so you can come back real quick."

Miss Fletcher shook her head. "Ida, she's had a stroke. Even if she does recover, more than likely I'll need to stay and help take care of her."

Ida averted her eyes. "I suppose it's selfish of me, Miss Fletcher," she said, once again resisting tears, "but I so wanted to go on and be a teacher. Like you."

Miss Fletcher managed a smile. "Ida, how long have I been your teacher?"

"Five years."

"And you've been my best pupil. Even if you put it off awhile, you'll make a fine teacher."

Ida stared at her hands. "But I *can't* wait. You see, up at our farm, it's been a good year. My folks said if I passed and if I found a family I could board with in town, I could continue my schooling. They might be able to afford that, this year." She looked up. "Miss Fletcher, I love my parents. I just don't want to be a sheep farmer my whole life."

"Ida, I wish it could be otherwise."

There was a noise. Ida glanced up. Tom was standing by the door. She wondered how much he had heard.

Miss Fletcher turned. "Tom," she said, "please call an end to recess."

"Yes, ma'am." He walked out.

Ida started to go back to her regular seat. She was halfway there when she paused. "Miss Fletcher, do you think girls don't need a high school education?"

"Oh no, of course I don't believe that. Mr. Jordan was not . . . thinking."

"It's what he said."

Miss Fletcher sighed. "Ida, do try to be patient."

"It's hard being patient," Ida replied, "if there's nothing to be patient for."

At day's end Ida opened the Ford's door and flung in the empty syrup can. She was about to call Felix to get him to take his place by the pedals when Tom came over.

"Tom Kohl," Ida said, "I'm still peeved at you."

"Why?"

"Suggesting I should just have fun instead of

being serious about my studies. You sounded like old toady Jordan."

"I was only trying to cheer you up," Tom said.

"You didn't."

"Hey," he said, pushing his hair out of his eyes, "I know I wasn't supposed to be listening, but I heard what Miss Fletcher said."

"And you called *me* a sneak-peek!"

"Said you'd be a good teacher."

"Never going to get the chance," Ida said.

"I thought of a way you could."

"How?"

"You could become our teacher."

Ida stared at him. "Just what is that supposed to mean?"

"You're such a gravy know-it-all," Tom said. "*You* could take over the school when Miss Fletcher leaves. Look, your legs weren't long enough to reach your car pedals, right? So you figured how to get Felix to work them."

"So what?"

"You might drive like a half-inch inchworm, but you're getting to school a lot faster than you used to, aren't you? Same thing here. Just have to find a way. And the way is, you be our teacher."

Ida glared at him. "Are you telling me what to

do?" Annoyed, she turned away from him. "Felix," she yelled, "come on!"

While she held the car door open, her brother squirmed into the cab and onto the floor. Then Ida got in and tied the door shut.

Not saying a word, Tom went to the front of the car, ready to crank up the motor as he usually did at the end of school when Ida and Felix went home.

A frowning Ida sat behind the steering wheel and set the spark lever—on the left side of the steering wheel—to the third notch, then fixed the throttle lever—on the right side of the wheel—on the fifth notch.

"Neutral," she said to Felix.

Below, Felix pushed the clutch pedal down.

"Ready," he said.

"Ready!" she called out to Tom, who turned the starter crank and gave the motor a couple of turns.

As the motor sputtered into motion, Ida adjusted the spark lever until the engine ran smoothly.

"Reverse!" she called to Felix, who pushed in the reverse pedal while she released the hand brake.

The car backed up and swung around, stopping

when Ida pulled back the brake lever. "Forward clutch!" she called.

Felix released the reverse clutch pedal, then pushed in the forward one.

"Let's go!" Ida shouted while shifting the throttle lever.

In moments the old Ford was bumping down the dirt road toward home.

"Ida!" Felix called up from beneath the dashboard after they had gone on awhile.

"What?"

"Is something wrong? Did Tom say something mean? What are you thinking about?"

"Nothing," Ida snapped. But in fact Tom's idea kept churning in her head.

Could I really become the teacher? she thought.

Three

꙳

As Ida parked the backfiring car in their farmyard driveway, bleating lambs, tails up, ran in fright, while Snooker, the old mare, looked over the corral fence.

"Felix," Ida whispered after they got out, "don't tell Ma or Pa what happened in school."

Felix's look turned quizzical. "How come?"

"I need to tell them my way. Understand?"

"No, but okay," he said, accepting, as always, his older sister's ways.

Ida opened the front door of their log cabin. It had been built by her father when he came from eastern Colorado years ago. At the time people thought there was gold in the surrounding mountains.

A red-faced Mrs. Bidson was in the steamy kitchen, stirring laundry atop the wood-burning stove. Baby Shelby was on her lap.

"Hi there!" she called. "How was school?"

"Fine," Ida said glumly.

"You sure?"

"Yes."

Felix darted a look at Ida. She put a finger to her lips. "Want some help with Shelby?" she offered.

"Just been waiting for you to come home," Mrs. Bidson said with a smile as she handed the baby over. "Felix, your pa's in the barn. Said to say you were needed soon as you got in."

Felix gulped down a glass of milk, then stuffed a hunk of bread into his mouth. Before racing away, he beckoned Ida over and whispered, "Why didn't you tell Ma that Miss Fletcher is leaving?"

"I'm not sure what I'm going to do."

He screwed up his face. "*Do?* What's that supposed to mean?"

"Tell you when I make up my mind."

Ida stayed with the baby for an hour, then got on with her regular chores. She mucked out the horse's stall and milked the cow. Working along with her father, she checked the early lambs, and finally, after she'd helped her mother with supper preparations, Ida set out the soaking barrels for the next day's laundry.

At supper Ida didn't say a word about school. Most of the talk was about a new hay field Mr. Bidson was thinking about fencing in.

That evening, up in the loft bedroom Ida and Felix shared, Ida put aside the year-old *Saturday Evening Post* she'd been reading, lay back, and stared up at the wooden plank roof. She liked to imagine different pictures for the grain patterns. It always soothed her. One night it was a map. Another time it was secret writing. Sometimes it was even music. Tonight it was the road to school.

But as soon as Felix was asleep, Ida slipped out of her bed and crept down the steps to the kitchen. Her mother was still awake, boiling baby bottles in a big pot.

"Hello, love," her mother said with a quick if tired smile. "Thought you'd gone to sleep a long time ago."

"Felix has. I couldn't."

"Something on your mind?"

Ida perched upon a chair and pulled her flannel

nightgown over her toes. "Can we talk?" she asked gravely.

Her mother continued working. "I'm listening."

"Where's Pa?"

"Out in the barn. The tractor motor is leaking. This girl talk?"

"It's school." Ida hesitated, then said, "Ma, Miss Fletcher's mother is very sick. On Wednesday she's leaving to go to Iowa to be with her."

"Oh dear!"

"And Mr. Jordan—he's head of the school board—"

"I know."

"—said they wouldn't replace her."

"For heaven's sake. Why not?"

"Said it was too late in the term." Ida paused. "I think he just wants to save money."

"Times *are* getting tight, honey. The valley doesn't have much money. I'm sorry about Miss Fletcher."

"I am, too, but they're closing the school for the year."

"Closing?"

"And Ma, the thing is, if school closes, it means Tom and I can't take the final exam."

"Oh, honey! And you've been working so hard."

"Ma, it's a lot more. No exam—no high school."

Mrs. Bidson thought for a moment. Then she said, "Ida, love, high school was only a possibility. Like we told you, your going depends on how we do on the farm, anyway. Year by year."

"I know."

Ida watched her mother pluck the baby bottles from the hot water and set them to dry. "Ma," she said after a moment, "you know what Tom said?"

"Guess I don't."

"He had an idea how we could keep the school going."

"How?"

"Said . . . I should be the teacher."

Mrs. Bidson looked around. "You mean, you . . . teaching?"

"Ma, I've been going to school almost forever. I guess I should know how to do it. And you know I've always wanted to be a teacher."

"Think they'd hire you?"

Ida shook her head. "Not for money."

"I don't understand."

"Just ... doing it."

Mrs. Bidson sat down, all attention now. "Honey, you're only fourteen. No one needs to tell me how smart you are. But think, if you were teacher, you'd have all that figuring out of the students' lessons, checking all their work, plus being in charge of the schoolhouse. It'd be hard making everyone mind, too. And you'd still have your own schoolwork to do on top of all that. What do the other children have to say?"

"Don't know. It was Tom's idea. I'd never even thought about it before he mentioned it."

"Well, Tom's sweet on you."

"Ma!"

"Course he is."

"Anyway, that doesn't have anything to do with it."

"Maybe," her mother said with a quick smile. "As for you teaching, I suppose it might work. But only if the other children went along. And I guess you'd need to speak to Mr. Jordan."

Ida winced. "Why him?"

"Like you said, Mr. Jordan's head of the school board. You'd need his permission, wouldn't you?"

Ida remained still for a moment. Then she said,

"I guess. But do you think I should even *try* being teacher?"

"You're set on trying to get to high school, aren't you?"

Ida nodded.

"And you need your exam to do it, right?"

Ida nodded again.

"Ida, your getting to high school would be a family first. But you got to keep in mind what your pa told you: If you go, we'd still need to pay for your room and board in town. And even though Felix is getting older, he's only seven. Keeping things running around here is going to be harder without you."

"I'd be home weekends."

"When the snow let you."

"Ma, it's just *now* I'm talking about. Maybe I won't tell Pa what I'm doing."

Mrs. Bidson frowned. "Not sure I like that. The point is, your chores won't ease up none even if you are the teacher. We need you pitching in here, too."

"But . . . do you think I *could* do it?"

"Being teacher, now, well, it would be un-usual, I guess. But most things seem so when they're new. I can't see how it would hurt you any."

"Think I'd be . . . good?"

"Ida, love, though your father's keen on reading, neither of us got much schooling. Bit of writing, sums. I think you'd be good. But . . . honey, it's not my world."

"I know," Ida said. Suddenly recalling that at five-thirty in the morning it would be milking time again, she said, "I better go to bed," and headed back to the loft.

"Ida!" Mrs. Bidson called after her.

Ida looked back.

"If you decide to do it, I'll give you something."

"What's that?"

"Hairpins," Mrs. Bidson said with a smile. "If you put up your hair, you'll look older."

Four

THE NEXT DAY DURING midmorning recess, Ida approached Tom. "I want to talk to you," she announced quietly. Without another word, she headed for the pond.

"Still angry at me?" Tom asked her when he caught up.

"I wasn't, really," she said. "Just upset about school, that's all."

"Me, too. When I told my folks they were hopping mad about it. Back in Germany, before they came here, they didn't get much learning. So they really hoped I'd go on to high school. Want me to be something different than they are."

At first Ida remained quiet. Then, shyly, she said, "I was thinking over what you said, about my being the teacher."

"You could do it."

"My ma said I'd have to ask Mr. Jordan."

Tom shook his head. "Old geezer would never agree."

"I know."

Ida looked up at Tom's long face, with its almost-but-not-quite turned-up nose. He seemed serious, too, but when he pushed his hair away from his forehead—a habit of his—Ida saw a gleam in his brown eyes.

"So if we did it," he said, smiling, "it'd have to be done in . . . secret. That what you're thinking?"

Ida nodded. "And that means all the rest would have to agree."

"You game to ask 'em?" Tom said.

Ida took a moment. "Yes," she whispered.

Tom grinned.

"We've got to plan for when Miss Fletcher goes," Ida said to the other kids as they ate their lunches of bread with jam or lard, meat slices, and apples.

"Already got my plan." Herbert laughed. "One long vacation and it starts day after tomorrow."

"You're always taking a vacation," Susie said.

Herbert flushed. "Am not! Working, that's what. My dad says there ain't no laws can force me to go to school. Unconstitutional."

"Look here," Tom cut in impatiently. "With Miss Fletcher gone and school closed, next year it'll be the same as if we all got held back a whole year."

"You mean repeat *everything?*" Natasha asked, aghast.

"You heard Mr. Jordan," Tom said. "School board won't bring in another teacher. Which means you get no credit for the year. And Ida and I won't get our exit tests."

"I don't like tests," Susie said.

Ida said, "It's just Tom and me who need them. But I bet you'd hate it a lot if you didn't get credit for your whole fourth grade."

"Yeah," Herbert said, "then you'd grow up to be a dumb old maid like Ida!"

Ida gave him a dirty look.

Charley said, "Then what are you fixing to do about it?"

Ida felt her heart beat faster. "Tom," she said, "had a notion."

Everyone looked at Tom.

31

"Who's the smartest of everybody here?" he asked.

For a moment no one said anything. Then Natasha said, "I'm the best speller. And you're best at math. But all in all, for high marks, I guess it's Ida."

"So I say," Tom said, "Ida should become our teacher."

"My own sister, the teacher?" Felix cried with such dismay everyone burst out laughing.

"I'm serious," Tom went on. "We have to have a teacher, right? Except Mr. Jordan said the school board won't get one till next year. But if we got one now and did our own schooling, everyone could move on to the next grade, and Ida and I could take our exams. She knows what to do. Let her be teacher."

"How you going to make sure we behave?" Herbert said with a grin. "Get out the switch?"

"Switch whipping is mean," Mary Kohl said.

"And I don't believe in it," Ida said.

"Then how?" Herbert challenged her.

Ida shrugged. "Find some way."

"Hey," Herbert said, "it'll be worth coming to school just to see you try."

Everyone laughed again.

"But," Natasha said earnestly, "what about the

school board? Think they'd let you? You know, pay and everything?"

"Wouldn't ask for pay," Ida said. "Do it for nothing."

"Mr. Skin-a-flint Jordan would love that," Herbert said.

"But the main thing is," Tom said, "because I bet the school board wouldn't let us do it, we won't ask. We'll just do it on our own."

"A *secret* teacher?" Felix asked.

"A *secret* school?" asked Mary.

"But," Natasha said with dismay, "I already told my parents school was going to close."

The other children nodded. They had, too.

Tom said, "Well, just tell them things got changed a little, that school *is* going on. Which it would be . . . mostly. No fibbing there."

"But what if they ask who's teaching?" Natasha asked.

"Say you don't know yet."

"People are going to find out at Last Day Exercises," Charley pointed out.

"Be too late by then," Tom said.

"Well, I do love secrets," Herbert said.

"All in favor, raise your hands," Tom said after a moment.

All eight hands shot up.

"Then I guess," Ida said, "I'm your teacher."

The decision made, the children sat there, waiting for Ida to say something.

"Just remember," she said softly, "this really does need to be a secret. Now go play."

When the other children ran off, Ida and Tom stayed behind.

Ida sighed. "I can't believe we're doing this."

"You nervous?"

"I think so."

"Know what my uncle once told me?"

Ida shook her head.

"Said, 'If you want to try something new, and you're not scared, means you're not really trying something new.'"

"Maybe I'm too scared," Ida said with a wan smile.

"Which scares you the most," Tom pressed, "teaching, or not going to high school?"

"I think I'd hate myself if I didn't try everything to get there," Ida said after a moment.

"Well," said Tom, "if I had to pick between hating myself and scaring myself, guess I know what I'd do."

"What?"

"Oh no!" Tom said, getting up. "Last time I suggested what you could do, you got mad at me. You're gonna have to decide for yourself." He grew thoughtful. "But if you do it, we still going to be friends?"

Ida blushed. "Tom Kohl!"

Tom grinned. "Just asking." He walked away, untied Ruckus, and led him to a shady spot to graze.

Ida watched Tom go and then strolled down to the little pond back behind the schoolhouse. On hands and knees, she studied her reflection in the still water. She was sure she didn't look like a schoolteacher.

After making sure no one was watching, Ida undid her braids, then pulled back her hair and looked at herself again. The Ida who gazed back at her now appeared a little older—a little more like a teacher.

The bell rang. Quickly, Ida rebraided her hair and ran back to school.

"Well?" Tom whispered to her when she slipped onto the bench, next to him.

"I'm going to be scared," Ida answered softly. "Very scared."

Five

WEDNESDAY AFTERNOON, shortly before three o'clock, Miss Fletcher said, "Children, please put away your work."

There was a quick rustling of papers and closing of books. Expectant, the children sat back on their benches.

Miss Fletcher walked solemnly to the front of her desk. Once there she clasped her hands. Briefly, she closed her eyes, then opened them.

"Children," she began, "as you know, this has been my last day. I just want to say that I have so much enjoyed my five years with you. I ... do hope the school board will make arrangements so your studies can continue next fall.

"Now, if you treat your next teacher with the same kindness and respect you've shown me, everything will—I'm quite sure—be fine."

There was some anxious shifting among the children. The two younger ones stole looks at Ida.

"And...," Miss Fletcher concluded in a slightly husky voice, "I guess you do know how much I love you."

There was a nervous hush. Then Ida stood up. "Miss Fletcher, the class has asked me to say some words."

"Well, yes, Ida. Thank you. You may."

Ida walked up to the recitation spot in the front of the room. Addressing the teacher, hands clasped together, she began: "Miss Fletcher, we, the pupils of the Elk Valley School, wish to thank you for your excellent instruction and generous attention. No matter where we go upon the long road of life, we shall hold you dear in our hearts and memories. By so doing we shall strive to live by the poem you taught us,

"Do what conscience says is right;
Do what reason says is best;
Do with all your mind and might;
Do your duty, and be blest."

Ida unclasped her hands. "Miss Fletcher, I . . . we . . . really liked you being our teacher."

Ida now turned to Mary Kohl, who was seated on the first bench. "Mary . . ."

Mary jumped up, ran to the girls' wardrobe, and returned with a small wicker basket covered with a blue cloth. Bobbing a curtsy, almost breathless with excitement, she presented the basket to the teacher. "We made this up for you," she said.

Miss Fletcher, her hands fluttering, uncovered the basket. Inside was a mason jar of jam, a cake, two apples, a bag of cookies, plus two pencils.

"We made everything," Mary explained. "Except the pencils. Charley boughten them."

Miss Fletcher wiped her eyes with her handkerchief and said, "It's so lovely! I will surely keep the memory of this forever. And I—"

From outside came the sharp beep of a car horn.

"Oh my!" the teacher cried. "It's Mr. Plumstead. He's being kind enough to take me to the train station."

The students rushed from their benches. Miss Fletcher, wiping away more tears, hugged the children one by one.

When Herbert approached, he held up the switch.

Miss Fletcher, taken aback, asked, "What's that for?"

Herbert grinned. "Don't you want to give me one more lickin' for good luck?"

Miss Fletcher laughed and hugged him hard. "Herbert Bixler, you are not a bad boy. You're not."

"Well," he said, clearly enjoying the hug, "I sure tried."

Outside the horn tooted impatiently.

"Felix, go tell Mr. Plumstead I'm coming!" Miss Fletcher cried. "Tom, Herbert, be kind enough to carry my trunk to his car. Charley, my portmanteau is by my desk. Mary, you shall carry my precious basket. Children, have you got your things? You mustn't forget your books and coats. You won't be able to get into school till next fall."

In a great flurry, Miss Fletcher locked the door.

The children exchanged looks.

"Miss Fletcher," Herbert asked, "want me to take care of the key?"

"Oh! No, thank you. I'll give it to Mr. Plumstead."

The teacher allowed herself to be escorted to

39

the waiting car. Mr. Plumstead, president of the Elk Valley Bank, loaded the luggage into the open rumble seat of his Studebaker, making a great fuss that it was done just right. Then he climbed into the driver's seat and looked at Miss Fletcher expectantly.

Miss Fletcher, reluctant to leave, stood before the children. "Oh, I do wish you all the very, very best," she said again. "Work hard. And—"

"Miss Fletcher," Mr. Plumstead called, "if you're going to catch the train, we're going to have to get moving."

"Yes, yes, I'm coming." The teacher opened the car door and settled in. "Good-bye, children!" she called as Mr. Plumstead put the car into gear and started off.

"Good-bye! Good-bye!" the students shouted.

They ran out into the road to watch the car go. Within moments it had disappeared from view, leaving behind only the faint smell of exhaust fumes.

Ida turned. The other seven children were staring at her.

"Ida," Susie whispered with alarm, "if the door is locked, how we ever going to get inside the school?"

"I've already thought of that," Ida announced. "Follow me!"

The children trooped after her until she stopped by a window on the west wall. "Tom, Herbert," she said, "you need to give me a hoist."

The two boys made a stirrup of their hands, and Ida stepped into it. Rising up, she slid open the window and, headfirst, squirmed inside. Within moments she reappeared at the window. "Meet me at the door," she called.

The children ran around to the front of the schoolhouse.

When the door didn't open right away, Herbert banged on it. "Hey, Ida! Come on! Open up!" he called.

The door swung in. There stood Ida. The children gasped. She had put up her hair with the pins her mother had given her.

"Children," she said in the most prim teacher-like voice she could manage, "school is closed for the day. It will open regular at eight-thirty sharp tomorrow morning."

There was a whoop of laughter.

"I am quite serious," Ida said firmly. "School is dismissed for the day." She closed the door.

The children looked at one another, surprised.

Gradually they drifted off, leaving only Felix. Not sure what to do, he sat down on the front steps.

The door opened behind him. Ida peeked out. "They all gone?"

"I guess you told them to, didn't you?"

"Tom, too?"

"Yeah."

Ida stepped off the porch. "Come on. Guess if we're going to get home we're going to have to crank up the car ourselves."

As they walked toward the car Felix looked up at his sister. "Ida . . ."

"What?"

"I like your hair better down."

"Well, you better get used to it," Ida said. "It's going to stay up."

Six

"HAVE TO GET TO school half an hour earlier tomorrow," Ida announced at the supper table.

"How's that?" her father asked between mouth-
fuls of bean and lamb stew.

"The new teacher starts," Ida said softly.

Felix stared at his sister.

Mrs. Bidson, who had been attending the baby
on her lap, looked up at Ida sharply.

"That school board's sure been quick getting a
replacement for Miss Fletcher," said Mr. Bidson.

"How did you know?" Ida asked faintly.

"Your ma told me about Miss Fletcher leaving," her father explained.

For a moment no one spoke. Then Mrs. Bidson reached out and touched Ida's hand. "Honey, don't you want to say more?"

Mr. Bidson looked up and gazed around at the somber faces. "Am I missing something?" he asked.

"Pa," Ida whispered, "I'm the new teacher."

Her father stared at her for a moment as if not understanding. He turned to his wife, then back to Ida. Putting down his fork, he said, "Better say that again."

Ida gripped the edge of the table with both hands. Then she said, "I'm Miss Fletcher's replacement."

"Only nobody knows," Felix piped in.

Mr. Bidson sat back and used his napkin to wipe his lips. "Ida Bidson," he said, "I'd sure be pleased to hear some more about this."

Ida gave a pleading look at her mother, who responded with a tiny nod of encouragement.

"Well...," Ida began, and gave a quick summary of what had happened at school, how her being the replacement teacher meant that she and Tom could take their final exams, it being the only way they could move on, and that this arrangement was agreed to by each of the children.

"I knew women got the vote," Mr. Bidson said with a slight smile, "but that go for kids, too?"

"We did vote," Felix said proudly. "Me, too."

Ida looked across at her father. "Is that okay with you?"

"The school board—with Mr. Jordan—gave permission?"

Ida stole another look at her mother. This time Mrs. Bidson gave no response.

"Pa," Ida pleaded, "he doesn't even think girls should go to high school."

Mr. Bidson made a dismissive wave of his hand. "Old Jordan's notion of progress is to close his eyes and step back to eighteen twenty-five."

"Pa," said Ida, "we're . . . not even telling him."

"It's a secret school," Felix announced solemnly.

Mr. Bidson, a flicker of a smile hovering over his lips, looked around at his wife. Then he grinned. "Kids, you have as much chance keeping secrets in the valley as you do growing oranges. But see here, Ida, my love, I won't quarrel none. I'm going to have to say something, though: The farm comes first. Before any high school."

Ida swallowed hard. "I understand."

Mr. Bidson nodded. "All right, then," he said. "Give it a try. I wish you luck."

"But it has to be a secret," Ida reminded him.

Her father laughed. "Won't even tell the sheep."

The next morning Ida got up at four-thirty, milked the cow, mucked the stall, and spread grain for the chickens. After a hasty breakfast, she pinned up her hair.

She and Felix got to school early.

"It's cold," Felix complained as he slid out of the car.

Ida yawned. "Let's fetch some wood. We'll light the stove." While Felix was loading up his arms with wood from the woodpile behind the school, Ida rolled a large log under the window. Then she stood on the log and crawled through the window.

Once inside she stood quietly and looked all around her. The one-room building seemed larger than usual.

Ida started toward the back-row bench. Catching herself, she moved to the teacher's desk. When she reached it, she stopped and touched the cool wooden surface. A chill went through her body.

Taking off her coat, Ida automatically moved toward the girls' wardrobe, only to catch herself again. She made herself use the teacher's hook. Then she had to force herself to sit in the teacher's chair. Once seated, she summoned up her will and gazed at the empty rows and desks before her.

"I'm fourteen years old and a dumb dora," she whispered out loud.

There was a knock on the door. Stomach queasy, holding her breath, Ida opened the door. It was only Felix.

"Hey Ida," he cried, "what took you so long? Give me a hand!" He staggered in under the load of wood.

"Felix," she replied, trying to control her voice, "though I'm still your sister and you may call me Ida at home, in school, henceforward, I'm your teacher and you must call me Miss Bidson." She took a few of the logs out of his arms.

Felix dropped the remaining wood in the wood box. Arms akimbo, he said, "That mean you're gonna talk like a teacher, too?"

"The proper words are *going to*."

Felix glared at her and then escaped outside.

At eight-thirty—though Ida wasn't too sure of the time because she belatedly realized that, unlike

47

Miss Fletcher, she did not have a pocket watch—she removed the school flag from the bottom drawer of her desk, then went to the door and pulled the cord to ring the bell.

The class gathered around the flagpole and raised the frayed flag. Then all seven children stormed inside. They were acting, Ida immediately realized, louder and more boisterous than when Miss Fletcher had been there. Increasingly unsure of herself, Ida went to her desk at the front of the room.

The school became quiet.

Everyone was staring at her. "Good morning, class," Ida said.

"Morning, Ida!" Herbert shouted out.

Feeling herself go red, Ida snapped, "Herbert Bixler, I'll ask you to remember my name is Miss Bidson."

"Oh yeah?" he said.

"Yes. Now again, good morning, students," Ida said.

"Good morning, Miss Bidson!"

Struggling not to panic, Ida tried desperately to remember all that Miss Fletcher and their other previous teachers had done to start the day. She must act, she told herself, as if she were in complete control. She only hoped that her dress would hide her shaky legs.

Suddenly she remembered: *Singing.* That was how they always began.

She cleared her throat. "As usual," she said, hoping she sounded confident, "we will begin the day with a song. Susie Spool, please lead us as you normally do."

The children stood, and Susie came to the recitation spot in front of the room and began to sing "Amazing Grace."

Her clear, firm voice filled the entire room, soothing Ida, and giving her time to think. On the second verse the other children joined in. Eyes closed, Ida sang along with all her heart.

By the time the song was finished, Ida had re-gained sufficient calm to say, "Thank you, Susie, for your lovely rendition. You may take your seat."

As Susie did so, Ida took a deep breath. She was feeling much better.

"Today," she said, "we shall begin as we always do. Mary and Felix will read to me from their primers. Tom—you'll study your mathematics, then assist Susie with hers. Natasha, you need to work on your geography. Charley, you'll parse the opening paragraph from *The Way to Be Happy,* page one-fifty-nine of your reader." To Ida's astonishment, the children reached for their books.

Then, from across the room Herbert called, "What about me?"

"Herbert Bixler, you will read your history."

"I'd sure like to see you make me," the boy said, a great grin on his face.

The room became deathly still.

Seven

❧

HERBERT LEANED OVER his desk and smirked at Ida. She was quite certain her pounding heart could be heard by everyone. The other children were looking down, except for Tom, who was frowning angrily at Herbert. Suddenly Tom stood up, hands balled into fists.

Herbert laughed. "Teacher's pet going to defend the teacher?" he taunted.

"Tom Kohl, sit down!" Ida cried. "I'm in charge."

A reluctant Tom sat, even as Ida, with unsteady legs, stood up. The children gazed at her. The younger ones, Mary and Felix, were wide-eyed with fright.

Momentarily, Ida glanced at the switch that hung close by on the wall. She knew she could not use it. It wasn't in her. Besides, she knew Herbert would only fight back. If that happened, it would be the end of school. No, she'd have to try something else.

She turned back to the class. "Herbert Bixler," she said, trying to be calm but not, she sensed, being very successful, "I asked you to study your history. Are you going to do it or not?"

Herbert only laughed, leaned back, and put his hands behind his head and his bare feet up on the desk in front of him. "Hey, Ida, I'm just saying you can try and make me if you want."

Ida, finding it hard to breathe, walked up the side aisle. Herbert watched her come but did not move. His grin had become frozen.

Drawing closer to the boy, Ida said, "Herbert Bixler, are you going to do as you're told?"

"Guess I'll do what I want, thank you, ma'am," he replied, trying to sound flippant.

A deep anger went through Ida. Herbert would spoil everything. If she couldn't control him, the school would not work. "Does anyone," she snapped, "make you come to school?"

"Come only if I want," Herbert retorted, but her unexpected question brought an edge of uncertainty to his voice.

"Everyone in this room is wanting to learn," Ida said. "We all took a vote to keep this school open, so I guess we can pretty well vote you out if we want. Then the whole valley will know you for what you are, a skulking, low-down, lazy dud."

Laughter rippled through the room. This was not regular teacher's talk. The grin on Herbert's face turned sickly.

Gaining strength, Ida cried, "Is that what you want? To be known as a lazy dud?" She made a sharp bang on the floor by stamping her foot. Everyone jumped.

"I ain't saying—," Herbert said as he pulled his feet back from the desk.

"I don't care what you *say*," Ida snapped furiously. "I'm only caring for what you *do*!"

She turned to the class. "All right, students. We'll take a vote. Those in favor of forever expelling Herbert Bixler from—"

Herbert sat up. "Hey, Ida, I was only fooling!"

"What's my name?"

"Aw . . ."

Ida went on, "All in favor of expelling Herbert Bixler from this school if he ever interferes again, raise your hands."

She lifted her own hand. The other hands shot up. "Majority rules," she announced, turning back to the boy. "You either do as I tell you or you're expelled."

Herbert's face turned red. "Hey . . . Miss Bidson . . . I was just joshing," he mumbled.

"Take out your history book," Ida commanded.

"Yes, Miss Bidson." Sheepishly, Herbert pulled out his old book, opened it, and bowed his head over the pages.

Feeling enormous relief, Ida looked around. Tom gave her a wink.

Ida blushed and nodded curtly, then returned to the teacher's desk. She felt exhausted. And the day had only just begun.

"Mary and Felix," she said softly after a moment of silence that seemed to last forever, "you may come and read to me now."

As the two youngest came forward, readers in

hand, the room's tension melted. The others turned to their tasks.

It was midmorning when Ida suddenly realized it must be recess time. She made the announcement.

The children dropped their work and rushed outside, except for Tom.

"Aren't you going out?" Ida asked.

Tom remained seated on his bench. "Am I going have to call you Miss Bidson, too?" he asked.

Ida, suddenly fearful she might cry from the morning's tension, turned away. "Yes," she said.

Tom gazed at her, then headed for the door.

"Tom," Ida suddenly said, "it's a whole lot harder than I thought. I don't know if I can do it."

He smiled. "You're doing fine . . . Miss Bidson."

"Thank you," she said stiffly.

"Going to take recess?"

Ida sighed. "Teachers never do."

At the door, Tom paused. "Miss Bidson," he said, "don't go forgetting who you are. It'll make it harder for you. And your friends."

Eight

AFTER RECESS SCHOOLWORK resumed. Mary and Felix did more reading. Then Ida asked that they work on math, with help from Tom. Meanwhile, she worked with Charley on his parsing exercises. Natasha sat with Herbert and helped him with his math, since he was behind. Susie, off by herself, worked on her penmanship.

As the day progressed, Ida felt her anxiety fade. She looked over the class. Everything was calm. School, to her surprise, was working. Then why was she so exhausted? Was every day going to be like this?

She tried to make a mental calculation as to

how much longer the term would be. To her horror, she realized she was too tired to even add properly.

Tom raised his hand.

"Yes, Tom?"

"Miss Bidson, may I come to the desk?"

"Of course."

Standing next to her and shielding his hand with his body, Tom showed Ida the face of his pocket watch and whispered, "It's past three."

A blushing Ida hastily dismissed the school.

"How'd it go?" her father asked her in the barn as she milked the cow later that afternoon.

"It was really hard," Ida confessed. "That Herbert Bixler acted up."

"Did you have to take the switch to him?"

Thinking of what happened, Ida suddenly found herself smiling. "Got him to work without it."

"Good for you."

"But the day seemed so long. Pa, I didn't even know the proper time to dismiss everyone. Don't have a watch. Tom had to tell me."

"I've got something for that." He left the barn and returned in moments with an old wind-up clock. It was ticking loudly.

Ida wrinkled her nose. "It's awful noisy," she said, not wanting to be unappreciative.

"Got a drawer in that teacher's desk of yours?"

"Yes."

"Keep it in there. And tell you what: I'll give you a good fleece to wrap it up in, too. That way no one will hear."

"Thank you," Ida said, giving her father an appreciative hug.

Much to Ida's surprise, Friday went smoothly. True, Herbert didn't come to school and Ida did wonder—considering what had happened—if he would ever come back.

Still, it was a relief to get to the weekend. She and her father dug holes and set in the posts on their way to extending the south meadow. She found the hard work soothing.

On Monday Herbert was back in school, acting as if nothing had happened, with no explanation about his absence, either. Though he was not always attentive and spent a great deal of time simply staring out the windows, he was no longer disruptive. Ida was content with marking him present in the attendance book.

She tried her best to follow how Miss Fletcher

had organized everything. Each day she had everyone read and memorize from their fifteen-year-old set of *McGuffey's Eclectic Readers*. She read aloud, too, a section a day from Charles Dickens's *A Tale of Two Cities,* from where Miss Fletcher had left off. They reviewed bits of geography (names of states, capitals, and rivers) and went over the facts of United States history (names of presidents in order, famous battles, important heroes). They did penmanship, bookkeeping, and grammar exercises—which meant parsing sentences or doing problems on the blackboard. Math problems were done, too, often out loud. Singing selections from the *Old Favorites Song Book,* plus recitations of memorized literature passages, rounded out the day.

On Friday afternoon the weekly contests were held, with Natasha Golobin, as usual, setting down all others in spelling. Tom won in mathematics. Ida added HIGH MARKS for both in the school ledger.

As Ida moved into her second full week of teaching, she caught herself taking moments to relax, gaining a growing awareness that she did not have to be teaching each and every minute of the day. An even bigger discovery was that if she just let the students work at their own pace and allowed their questions to become discussions for the class, time went by quickly. More and more she found herself listening to them, thinking about what *they* said, rather than worrying about what she should say.

It amazed her, too, how much she saw from the teacher's desk. Things she had never noticed before. Like how Felix screwed up his eyes when concentrating, or the way Natasha chewed her pencil, or how often Mary put her head down and napped. Or even how Tom fiddled with his right earlobe whenever he read intently.

One afternoon right after lunch, Tom raised his hand.

"Yes, Tom?"

"Miss Bidson, I brought something in that everyone might like to listen to."

"Listen to?"

The whole class turned around to see what Tom was talking about.

Reaching down, Tom brought out a box, placed it on his desk, opened it, and pulled out something Ida had never seen before. It looked like a snarl of wires.

"What is that?" she asked.

Tom, beaming, held it up. "A crystal radio. I built it myself."

"A radio!" Charley cried. "My dad says we're going to get one soon. Can I go look at it?" he asked Ida.

"Tom," Ida said, "why don't you bring it up here."

Proudly, Tom carried the apparatus to the teacher's desk. There was a scramble as the other students left their benches to gather around. Ida looked on, too.

The crystal radio consisted of a cardboard tube that looked like an oatmeal container around which copper wire had been carefully wound. Wires ran from the tube to a metal clip that held a shiny stone. There was also a hooked wire that looked like a tiny pointer. Attached to this thing was more wire, which was connected to a round disk.

"How's it work?" Herbert asked.

"Got to get this up first," Tom announced. He attached a long coil of wire to his radio and fed it out the window.

"Let's everybody go outside," Ida called.

The children scrambled for the door.

Once outside Tom handed Herbert the wire. "This is called an antenna. It pulls in the signal. You need to tie it up to the bell steeple."

Herbert took the wire, clenched it in his teeth, then got up onto Tom's shoulders and scrambled onto the roof. In moments he reached the steeple. Ida and the rest of the class cheered.

Herbert fastened the wire to the steeple, then reached in and clanged the bell. "School's out!" he called.

Everyone laughed.

As soon as he got down they all trooped back inside.

Tom began to fiddle with his radio. "You have to be very quiet," he said. "The mountains make reception hard."

"What's *reception*?" Felix asked.

"What you hear from a radio."

Tom picked up the round disk and held it to his left ear. "An earphone," he explained. With his right hand he manipulated the little pointer, poking it at different spots on the shiny stone—the crystal.

In breathless silence, everyone watched Tom as his face—earphone pressed to his ear—grew very intense. Suddenly he grinned. "Got KJQ," he announced. "Salt Lake City."

"Where's that?" Felix asked.

"Over in Utah," Tom explained.

"And what's KJQ mean?" Natasha asked.

"It's the radio station's call letters. Their name. They're playing music. I think it's called jazz. Does anyone want to hear—oops, it's gone."

"Where'd it go?" Charley asked in bewilderment.

"*Shhh!*" Tom commanded. He fiddled with the little pointer on the stone. "Got Denver! KDL!"

"What are they doing?" Ida asked.

Tom's face showed intense concentration. "Giving livestock prices. Here, listen!" He held out the earphone and put it flat against Ida's ear.

"...pork bellies are listed at twenty-two per..." she heard in a very scratchy voice, which faded, then grew louder. She handed the listening disk to Herbert, who then passed it on after a few minutes. One by one the children listened raptly. At one point Felix cried, "They're talking about sheep!"

After they'd each had a turn, Ida asked, "How does it work?"

Everyone attended closely while Tom went

into a complicated explanation of the workings of the radio. As he talked, Ida studied his face, deciding that what she liked most was its intensity. She loved how excited he was by what he had done.

Then they listened to the radio some more, continuing to pass the disk around.

As Tom poked different places on the crystal, each student would call out the locations. "Kansas City!" "Albany!" "Spokane!"

"We can go anywhere!" Felix cried excitedly.

Ida had the idea of pulling down the map of the United States and, using a pointer, indicating where each place they listened to could be found.

It was during Charley's turn that the most exciting moment occurred. "It's a baseball game!" he shouted. "From Chicago!"

Then it was time for afternoon recess. Ida had to almost shoo the younger kids out. Only she and Tom remained in the room.

"I'm glad you brought that in," she told him, as he packed the crystal radio away. "How'd you learn to make it?"

Tom gave a shy shrug. "*Popular Mechanics*. I wrote away for the parts."

Ida felt a swell of pride for him.

Suddenly the door burst open and a red-faced Mary Kohl appeared. "Ida...Miss Bidson," she corrected herself. "There's a lady out there I ain't never seen before. Says she's from the...County Education Office. Says she needs to meet with our teacher!"

Nine

❦

A TALL WOMAN STEPPED into the school. She wore a green felt hat and a black suit, the skirt reaching below her knees. A large purse dangled from one hand. Behind her the children crowded into the room.

Ida instantly recognized the woman as Miss Sedgewick from the County Education Office. She lived in Steamboat Springs—where the high school was—twenty miles down the valley. From time to time Miss Sedgewick came to their school to do inspections. And it was she who gave the exit exams.

Ida wondered if the woman would recognize her.

As she looked at Miss Sedgewick, Ida suddenly became aware of how shabby she must look in her simple polka-dot dress made over from one of her mother's. And the others looked just as ragged: Felix in baggy trousers; Tom, his shirt torn at the elbow; Herbert in old overalls, ripped shirt, no shoes on his feet; the other children no better. She remembered her ma saying how poor the valley was.

For a moment the children and the woman just scrutinized one another. Then she turned to Ida, whose heart was pounding.

"My name," the woman said, extending a white-gloved hand, "is Miss Sedgewick. From the Routt County Education Office. Where's Miss Fletcher?"

"She's gone," Ida managed to say.

"Gone? For the day?"

"For good."

"Oh?"

"Her mother, back in Iowa, got ill," Natasha said.

"I'm sorry to hear it," said Miss Sedgewick. "When was this?"

"Couple of weeks ago," Ida said.

"I see. And . . . who are you?"

"Miss Bidson is our new teacher," Mary called out.

"I see. Well, your school board was very fortunate to have found you so quickly, Miss Bidson, and to secure your services. I'm very pleased to meet you."

"Thank you, ma'am," Ida replied.

"No doubt the board will be forwarding your credentials to the county office." Miss Sedgewick paused, a look of puzzlement on her face. "Have we met before?"

"Not really," said Ida.

"Well, it'll be me, come June, who examines your eighth-grade-level students for their exit diploma. How many will there be?"

"I'm in eighth grade, Miss," Tom said quickly.

"Excellent," said Miss Sedgewick. "Your name?"

"Tom Kohl."

Miss Sedgewick took out a pencil and notebook from her purse and wrote down Tom's name. "Tom, you'll need to study hard. It's a challenging examination." She turned back to Ida. "Miss Bidson, is this your first teaching appointment?"

"Yes, ma'am."

"I confess, you seem very young," Miss Sedgewick said with a little laugh. "But I'm afraid that only tells you how my own years are getting on."

"Yes, ma'am."

Miss Sedgewick held up her notebook. "Might you tell me your full name?"

"Ida. Ida Bidson."

There was a moment of nervous silence as Miss Sedgewick wrote the name in her book. "Well, now," she said, looking about, "everything looks in perfect order. I'll not interrupt further. Miss Bidson, I'm very glad to make your acquaintance. Children, mind your teacher. Young man," she said to Tom, "I'll see you in a few weeks."

With a wave she walked out of the room.

From the doorway Ida watched Miss Sedgewick move toward her car. The other children looked on silently.

"Ida," Tom said softly behind her back, "if that lady doesn't know you need to take the test, she won't give it to you in June."

The moment Tom spoke, Ida knew he was right.

"Miss Sedgewick!" Ida called.

The woman paused and looked back.

"I need to speak to you," Ida cried.

"Yes, Miss Bidson?" the woman said as Ida approached.

The other children followed.

"Miss Sedgewick," Ida said breathlessly, "I'm . . . I'm not really a teacher."

"I beg your pardon?"

"I'm only in eighth grade," Ida rushed on. "When Miss Fletcher left, the school board decided to close down the school till next fall term because they said there wasn't enough time to get a new teacher."

"Close down the school?"

"Yes, ma'am. But we all"—Ida gestured to the others—"wanted to go on. Specially Tom. And me. So we can take our exit exams and go to the high school in Steamboat. We voted, ma'am—it was unanimous—to have me as teacher."

Miss Sedgewick studied the faces looking up at her. "Miss Bidson, exactly how old are you?"

"Fourteen, ma'am."

"I see. And you said you are in eighth grade?"

"Yes, ma'am."

There was a long moment of silence.

Then Felix blurted out, "She's my sister, but she's really smart."

"Pretty tough, too," Herbert put in.

"And she's a really good teacher," Natasha added. "She knows everything to do."

"I'm sure Miss Bidson has every one of those qualities," Miss Sedgewick said pensively. "But I need to understand something. While you and your classmates have gone on with the school—and with you as teacher, Miss Bidson—I trust you've informed the local school board what you are doing."

No one spoke. All eyes were on Ida.

"No, ma'am," Ida said very quietly.

"Ah. But what about your parents?" Miss Sedgewick said, addressing the group. "Have you informed *them* about what you are doing?"

Once more silence followed Miss Sedgewick's question.

"My parents know I'm teaching," Ida said at last.

No one else spoke.

"Well!" the woman exclaimed. "I've been with the county for fifteen years and I've never heard anything quite like this. It's most . . . unusual."

"I hope to be a real teacher someday," Ida said hurriedly. "But to do that, I have to get to high school first."

"Plus a year at the State Normal College in Greeley, I must add," Miss Sedgewick said rather primly.

"So this," Ida went on, "was the only way we—Tom Kohl and me—could think to keep the school going." She paused, then asked, "Can I... Can we... keep doing it? And... take the test?"

"Miss Bidson," Miss Sedgewick said, no longer smiling, "I think it's wonderful that you..." She paused. "But school boards act independently. My office has the duty to oversee teacher certification, curriculum, and exit exams. So... I'll have to look into this," she said with sudden abruptness. "You'll hear from me shortly."

With that, Miss Sedgewick, without another word, got into her car and drove off.

"Oh, you're going to get into trouble now," Herbert said.

"What do you think she'll do?" Tom asked Ida.

"Don't know," Ida said. "Has anyone—besides me—told their parents that I'm the new teacher?"

No one admitted to it.

"Best hold your tongues. Now, recess is a long time over," Ida announced, and headed back inside.

For what was left of the afternoon, the mood was anxious.

As Ida was getting into the car to head home, Tom went up to the front. He bent over to start cranking, but then stood up.

"What do you think is going to happen?" he asked.

"Don't know."

"I think you're doing a good job," he told her.

"Thank you," she said. "But, Tom, I don't think that'll have anything to do with it."

"It should," he said.

As Ida drove off—with Felix at the pedals— she recalled the places they had heard on the radio: Salt Lake City, Albany, Spokane, Chicago. In one day the world had become so big. But Elk Valley had never seemed so isolated.

Ten

IN THE DAYS FOLLOWING Miss Sedgewick's visit, the children often discussed—in worried terms—what the county inspector might do. Then when the woman did not return, their anxiety faded.

Ida tried to put it out of her mind, too—but with less success. She realized now that she couldn't be satisfied if just she and Tom took and passed their tests. She had an obligation to make sure that *everyone* did well.

A few days after that realization, Ida sat at her desk and tried to take the students' measure while they worked quietly.

Mary was behind in reading. Natasha was ahead. Should she review Natasha's progress before allowing her to go on to the next higher-level reader, or should she concentrate on Mary? Herbert continued to be absent a lot, and he didn't work much when he was there. He was slipping further and further behind. She tried to help him, but he was the only one in the class who didn't seem interested in learning. Charley was not achieving much, either—Ida was not sure why—but there he was every day, struggling. As for Felix, he was trying hard to succeed for his sister. Flourishing, too. Ida was grateful.

And Tom? He was working steadily, wanting, she knew, to do well in her eyes. But she had become more his teacher and less his friend. It didn't feel right. And Ida didn't know what to do about it.

She picked up a grammar exercise that Natasha had done. Even as she looked at it, red marking pencil in hand, she thought of her own studies. She was slipping behind. The problem was, there was so little time for herself. Each day ended with her getting home late, doing her chores, eating dinner, and grading schoolwork. Only then did she do her own studying, at least until she could no longer keep her eyes open.

Every day seemed the same, and every day she was growing more exhausted. And further behind. Could she be content if Tom passed and moved on to high school while she stayed back?

Her mind continued wandering until she noticed that Tom was raising his hand. "Yes, Tom?"

"Miss Bidson, I'm having trouble with this," he said, holding up a reader.

Ida went to his bench and took her old place beside him.

Tom, grinning shyly, slid his reader over. It was open to an excerpt from Shakespeare, from the play *Julius Caesar.*

"I don't think I get it," Tom said.

Ida stared at the passage. "Friends, Romans, countrymen," it began, "lend me your ears." It was a memory passage required of every eighth grader. In fact, Ida had heard it so often she had memorized it in fifth grade. How, she wondered, could Tom not know it? *He must be trying to get my attention,* she thought, and didn't know whether to be pleased or annoyed.

"How," Tom asked, "can you lend your ears to someone?"

Ida read and then reread the passage to herself as Tom waited patiently.

"I suppose," she finally, if cautiously, said, "it means he just wants them to listen."

"Oh. That all?"

Ida slid the book back to him. "Do you think?" she asked.

"You're the teacher," he said. "What you say, goes."

Ida blushed, then rose from the bench and returned to her desk.

The next morning an hour before dawn, Ida heard her mother call up the ladder, "Ida, honey, it's past milking time!"

Ida bolted up. Before she climbed down the ladder, she glanced at Felix, still asleep.

He looks so peaceful, she thought with a twinge of envy.

Wearing a pair of her father's rubber boots, she went to the barn. A low-burning lantern hung from a stall peg. Crisp air clouded her breath. The air was thick with the smell of cow and sheep.

Sitting on a stool with her mother's shawl over her thin dress, Ida pressed her face against the rough, warm belly of Bluebell and milked her. As Ida squirted the milk into the pail rhythmically, she thought of all the problems that lay before her.

But the big problem was that she was so tired. Teaching was much more exhausting than she ever thought it would be. She wanted to be young again, like Felix. Felix was content to do what he was told and was capable of plodding on cheerfully, eager for hard work or fun, no matter which.

Suddenly Bluebell slapped Ida in the face with her wet tail. With a start, Ida looked up. There was light in the sky. She was really late. And filthy. Pail in hand, she ran for the house and tripped, landing on her knees in the mud. The milk sloshed away, wasted.

"Pa," Ida said wretchedly when she went into the sheep barn to tell her father what had happened, "I'm no good at anything!"

Her father sighed and gave her a hug. "I suppose I could tell you everything's going to be all right," he said, "but you're too old for that."

Ida, to her own surprise, felt stung by his remark. "What's going to happen?" she asked.

"Happen?"

"To me."

"Honey," her father said, "think of what you're trying to do: the work around here, your teaching, moving on with your own studies, and I guess just being yourself. You've taken on a whole lot."

"Spilling the milk was an accident."

"Sure it was. But you were rushing. You've got too much on your mind. Lord knows, living round here is a full-time job. Lambing. Spring shearing coming up. Culling. Fence work. Cooking. Cleaning. Fixing. Planning. It ain't ever done."

"Should I stop teaching?" Ida asked in a small voice.

"Sweetheart, when you choose a hard way, it's going to be hard. No harm in admitting to a mistake."

"But I want to go to high school!" Ida cried.

"Ida, I'm going to remind you again that's not a sure thing. Even if you do get in, we'll need to find you a place to board. You know we might not have the money."

Ida hung her head.

"Ida, love, it's never mean to tell the truth."

She said nothing.

"Ida . . . ," he went on gently, a hand on her shoulder. Her head was still bowed. "How do you want to be treated, like a kid or a grown-up?"

The question startled her, and so, even more,

did her lack of a ready answer. She looked up into her father's face. It was the same as always, but for the first time she saw a hint of sadness in it. "I don't know," she confessed softly.

"Honey, that makes two of us," he said.

Ida pulled herself away and gathered up the empty milk pail. In the barn she carefully washed it out, then turned it upside down to drain dry. Her father would scald it later.

Back in the house she went up to the loft and dressed herself for school. Then she woke Felix.

They were late in leaving. Felix tried to talk, but Ida kept shushing him up. "Got to plan the day," she snapped. Her head ached.

By the time they drove up to the school, everybody except Herbert was there. Someone had already gone through the window and opened the door. Ida rushed inside.

On her desk was an apple. Seeing it, she stopped short, overcome with a flood of emotion. Leaving an apple was something she had done for *her* teachers. Did that mean—despite her faults, her tiredness—they thought she was doing a good job?

The day began as usual with flag raising. Then,

just before lessons started, Ida said, "Someone left me an apple. Thank you. May I ask . . . who it was?"

At first no one raised a hand. Then, rather bashfully, Tom did.

Ida felt herself blush. Of all the people in the room, the one person she didn't want thinking of her as just a teacher was Tom.

"She don't even like apples," Felix blurted out.

"Felix!" Ida cried.

Everyone laughed.

Ida stammered another thank you.

Then with a start she realized the class was waiting for her to begin.

"Susie Spool," she asked tremulously, "will you lead us in a song?"

Eleven

THAT FRIDAY, BECAUSE Herbert had been out of school for three successive days, Ida decided to visit him.

She didn't tell anyone what she was doing, not even Felix. When she drove away from school that afternoon, she simply turned the car to the right instead of the left. The Bixler farm was two miles south down the valley.

"Brake and clutch!" she called to Felix after the short ride. She stopped the car, but kept the motor running. Cranking it up on her own was very hard.

"Why are we stopping?" Felix asked.

Ida untied the door. "We're at the Bixler farm," she announced.

"What we doing here?" Felix wanted to know as he squirmed out from under the dashboard.

"I want to see if Herbert is all right," Ida said as she stepped down.

"Is something the matter with him?"

"I don't know. Thought I'd better find out why he's not been at school. You wait here."

The road where she had parked ran along a slight bluff. The Bixler farm was below her, cradled by a curve in the road. While Ida didn't exactly know how big the place was, she knew a poor farm when she saw it.

There was one small house, its wooden sides gray with weather and the remnants of red paint. Not far from the dilapidated porch was a rusty truck. It had no wheels and seemed to be permanently mired in the ground. There were two other pieces of farm equipment, both quite rusty. The remains of a child's swing hung from a cottonwood tree, its two frayed rope strands dangling.

Some thirty yards from the house was the barn. It was fairly large, but its main doors were lopsided and, from all appearances, permanently open. Over the doorway hung the bleached skull of an elk, its white antlers extended like long fingers of ice.

In the small corral in front of the barn stood a horse. A leggy young colt hovered close by, the only new thing in sight. Herbert was not to be seen nor, for that matter, was any other human.

There was a sense of disorder about the farm. Surely not the way Ida's father ran things. Ida wondered if it was a good idea for her to even be here.

As she hesitated, a man strolled out of the barn. Ida recognized him immediately as Herbert's father, Mr. Bixler. He wore rubber boots, rather dirty clothing, and a straw Western-style hat on his head. His face, what she could see of it, was hidden by a shaggy gray mustache.

"Howdy," he called, looking up to where Ida stood. He touched his hand to the brim of his hat in a gesture of polite greeting even as he poked the pitchfork tines into the earth, then leaned on it. "Can I help you, ma'am?"

"I'm...Ida Bidson," Ida called down. "I'm Herbert's...classmate."

"Are you, now?"

"Yes, sir."

"And what's bringing you here?"

"His...teacher wanted to know if he was all right."

"Did she? I'm sure I told Miss Fletcher it wasn't none of her business where my boy is. That she wasn't to come asking for him no more. She didn't ask you to come here, did she?"

Shocked by Mr. Bixler's words, Ida stammered, "No. Not...really."

"Then what you doing here?"

Ida didn't know what to say.

"Aren't you a bit young to come a courting?" he asked dryly.

Ida blushed. "No, I'm actually...his teacher," she blurted out, only to instantly regret her words.

Momentarily, Mr. Bixler glanced toward the barn. Then he looked back at Ida. "What happened to Miss Fletcher?" he asked her.

"She left," Ida said, wishing she had never come.

"Did she?"

"Her mother got ill," Ida said. Now, dimly, she saw Herbert standing deep in the interior of the barn. Hidden by the shadows, he stood motionless.

"Just how old are you, anyway?" Mr. Bixler asked.

"Fourteen."

"I see," Mr. Bixler said with care. There was no anger in his voice, just a dry tone that was burdened with a sad and weary weight. "You Noah Bidson's daughter?" he asked.

"Yes, sir."

"And you're playing at teacher, are you?"

"We're not *playing,* Mr. Bixler," Ida said with growing frustration. "We're trying to do things properly. And since I...I am his teacher, I was wondering about Herbert. He hasn't been to school lately. We've missed him."

"That right? Look here, Miss Ida, as I told that Miss Fletcher, Herbert is sorely needed around here. Schooling, I'm afraid, comes second to this farm, specially now that I hear it's just a play school."

"Mr. Bixler, it's not a—" Ida started to protest.

"Excuse my interruption, miss, but did you get the school board's approval for what you're doing?"

"I—"

"Miss Ida, the truth is, schooling just hasn't much to do with what's here." Mr. Bixler again touched his hat with his hand. "So I'd be much obliged if this was your last visit. Otherwise I just might have to visit Mr. Jordan and let him know

86

what's going on." Without another word, he turned and headed for the barn.

Ida was certain she saw Herbert dive away, back into the barn's interior.

For a moment she stood there, angry at Mr. Bixler but angrier still at herself. Had she given everything away? Worried, she ran back to the car and all but jumped into the seat.

"What's the matter?" Felix asked.

"Nothing," Ida snapped. "Let's get on home. Chores are waiting."

As she drove she went over what had been said, getting more and more worried. Then, three miles from their home, she called out, "Brake, clutch!"

Abruptly, she swung the car down a side road.

"Where we going now?"

"Got to see Tom."

"Why?"

"I need to speak to him."

They reached Tom's house in moments. The Kohls, like the Bidsons, were sheep farmers, and fairly successful ones. Where everything was shabby about the Bixler farm, the Kohl farm was neat and spruce. Beneath the soft shadows of Sand Mountain, buildings, fences, and machinery were all in good order.

Ida came to a jerky stop in front of the main house, where there was a long open porch. Mary was on the front steps, playing with three dolls. Tom was hunched over a table.

"Hey there!" he called. There were streaks of black over his face. His hands were dirty.

Ida let Felix out of the car, then climbed out herself. "I have to talk to you," she announced.

"You Miss Bidson or Ida?"

"Oh, Tom! Please don't."

"Come on up," he said with a grin. Felix, not waiting for an invitation, had already joined Mary on the steps.

Ida stepped onto the porch. On the table was some kind of small machine. There were lots of dirty sheets of paper about. "What are you doing?" she asked.

"Got me a little old printing press," Tom said. "My dad found it in the junk shop in town. I made myself some ink out of old crankcase oil and solvent. Got most of the letters. Just not enough Os. And it only does one page at a time."

"What are you printing?" Ida asked.

"Circular about a church supper. But what is it? You look all ragged."

"Tom," Ida said, "I just went to Herbert's place. Wanted to find out why he wasn't at school."

"His father keeps him close."

"I know. Mr. Bixler didn't know what we were doing at school. And by mistake . . . I told him."

"You did?"

"Tom, he said he might talk to Mr. Jordan. Think he will?"

"Don't know."

"But, if he does, what do you think will happen?"

Tom considered the question. Then, with a shrug, he said, "Guess your guess is as good as mine."

"You tell your folks?"

"Some."

"About me?"

"Well, yes."

"What did they say?"

Tom grinned. "Said they always figured you as smart."

Ida felt pleased but embarrassed. "Well, I'm *really* worried. Just hope I didn't ruin everything."

"Can't imagine you ruining anything."

Suddenly feeling shy, Ida turned and stepped off the porch. "Come on, Felix," she said brusquely. "We've got work at home."

Tom followed them to the car. "Thanks for coming by," he said.

"I'm sorry I can't stay," she said.

"Pretty busy," Tom said.

"I guess I am."

Tom bent over the crank.

Felix got in, then Ida. "Tom!" Ida called.

Tom stood up.

"Your farm, ours," Ida said, "they're so different than Herbert's. His was so . . . sad." Finding it difficult to say what she felt, she gripped the steering wheel hard. "Why do you think that has to be?"

"Don't know. Luck maybe. My old man says it's a different way of working. Maybe we'll learn all about that in high school."

She shook her head. "I wish I knew."

"Hey, Ida . . ."

"What?"

Tom pushed the hair away from his forehead. "Just want you to understand we all know how hard you're working. Can't be easy."

"Thank you," she said. "Felix, clutch."

Tom gave the motor crank a few turns.

Ida adjusted the spark and throttle, then called, "Clutch and brake!"

"We going home now?" Felix asked, as the car began to move.

"Yes," Ida said, watching Tom's image grow smaller in the rearview mirror.

Twelve

⚋⚋⚋

THOUGH IDA STILL HADN'T figured out how to be teacher, student, family member, and herself all at the same time, she found herself truly enjoying teaching. Each time she drove to school, she looked forward to what new things would happen.

As the days passed, she worked with or listened to each student separately, though there were times she worked simultaneously with two or three. When she wasn't spending time with them, the children were either learning lessons by themselves, memorizing, working with each other, studying together if they were on the same level, or helping one another if they were not. When they became tired or bored—which happened—they sat quietly, staring out the windows at the mountains, daydreaming. Sometimes they did little but listen to the other lessons that buzzed ceaselessly around them. Of course there were arguments, spats, even mean words—some of which brought tears. Once Herbert and Charley even got into a fight. Everything took sorting out.

Then there were school chores. Sweeping, mopping, cutting and hauling wood, dusting, taking out ashes, polishing desks, filling the stove, cleaning the privies, washing windows. Everybody did some of everything.

But with every passing day Ida felt more confident that things were truly going well. The children seemed to be working hard. She herself was not quite as exhausted as she had been. Even Herbert was in school more often than not. Maybe, after all, her visit had helped.

One afternoon as they were driving home, Felix said, "Ida, guess what Tom was talking about?"

"What?"

"That final exam you have to take."

"What did he say?"

"Said he's going to pass it easy."

Gritting her teeth, Ida said, "I hate that Tom Kohl," and immediately resolved to concentrate wholly on her *own* studies. But as soon as she arrived home, she was greeted by her father saying, "Ida, I need you in the barn." It was lambing season, an exciting but unsettled time. Newborns had a schedule all their own.

It was quite late when Ida finally crawled into her bed. She—working with her mother and father—had helped deliver twelve lambs. Spent, she lay down, only to realize she had done absolutely no schoolwork that night, neither for the students nor for herself.

She sat bolt upright. She *must* do something. Then Felix, across the room, gave a deep sigh in his sleep. He sounded so content, so utterly at rest, that Ida could do nothing but give way to her own tiredness.

Full of the pleasing sensation of willfully doing nothing, of being aware of nothing but her own body, she snuggled beneath her blanket. It seemed the sweetest thing to do in the whole world. In moments she was asleep.

Exactly two weeks after the day Miss Sedgewick had appeared, the weather turned springtime glorious. The air was balmy, with fluffy clouds floating through an arcing blue sky. The mountains themselves—with their constantly retreating snow-caps—seemed to be soaring. Tom announced he'd seen a bald eagle on the way to school. Charley countered by insisting he'd seen hummingbirds, the season's first. Early flowers—brilliant yellow snow lilies—dotted the valley, signaling spring's late arrival and the promise of summer, wonderful summer. No one, including Ida, wanted to be inside. Still, she told herself, they had to be.

All that morning, Ida kept stealing glances out the open window. Once, when she noticed Ruckus grazing, she even caught herself wishing she could be a mule for a day.

Four times she quietly opened her desk drawer, pulled the sheepskin aside, and checked the clock. She wasn't tired; she was restless. The room—despite the open windows—seemed small and stuffy.

When Ida caught sight of a mule deer coming down the road and then trotting off into the woods, she gave up. She had to get out, too. Suddenly she said, "I wish to make an announcement."

The fidgeting children gave her their attention.

"It's recess time and I've decided that I need recess, too. From now on I shall go outside and play when you do. When I do, I shall be Ida. But when recess is over, I will be Miss Bidson, your teacher, again. May we agree on that? All in favor, raise hands."

"Ida's gonna be a human again!" Herbert shouted as he stretched both hands high.

All the other hands shot up, too, and there was a dash for the door.

Once outside Ida didn't stop. Gathering her skirts in her hands, she ran as hard as she could—away from everyone, toward the eastern hills—as if determined to reach the top of a mountain. It felt so good to run again. Then she flopped down in the tall grass, spread her arms and legs like a windmill, and gazed up at the sky.

The sun was warm. The breeze in her face was fresh and clean. High above her, a hawk began to circle.

Ida giggled. *Maybe he thinks I'm a mouse,* she thought.

Suddenly consumed with a desire to play, she ran back to the school yard.

As soon as Tom saw Ida coming he huddled with Herbert. Then he called out, "Crack the whip! Crack the whip!"

Everybody tore down behind the privies to the flat area near the pond. Once there they all joined hands, urging Ida to be at the end. Completely giddy to be romping again, she agreed. It was Herbert who grasped her hand securely. Tom, being tallest, naturally took the lead. He led them round and round in tighter and tighter circles until Ida had a hard time staying on her feet. She didn't care. She was so happy to be part of the group again.

Tom led on, faster and faster, until, as he made the final cracking twist, he shouted, "Let her go!" With that, Herbert let Ida's hand slip. The boys had it all perfectly planned and timed. Ida went flying through the air until she landed, with a great splash, right in the middle of the pond.

Soaked and mud spattered, she sat in the water. For a moment she just remained there, gasping for breath, shocked. The next moment she broke out into laughter, laughing as she had not laughed in a long time. As the other children joined in, she could not stop.

Suddenly they heard a voice say, "My dear Miss Bidson. Are you giving swimming lessons?"

They looked around. It was the county examiner, Miss Sedgewick. She seemed to be struggling not to laugh herself. "I have visited many a school," she said, "but never one like this. Now I'm afraid I really do need to speak to you all."

Dripping wet, red faced, and mud streaked, Ida waded out of the pond and plodded in sodden shoes toward the schoolhouse. The other children followed uncertainly.

Tom edged up to Ida. "Sorry," he whispered.

She looked up at him. He looked so pathetically guilty that for a moment she felt an almost irrepressible giggle rising. "Do I look a sight?"

He hesitated for a moment, then said, "Yes," and started to laugh again but tried to repress it.

Ida bit her lip to keep herself from laughing more.

As the students filed into their places, Ida stood shivering beside the teacher's desk. This was, she knew, a very serious moment. Why was she so desperate to laugh?

"My dear," said Miss Sedgewick, "have you no dry clothes?"

"No, ma'am. Can I explain what we were—?"

"Miss Bidson, you *are* the teacher here. Do take your place."

Wet though she was, Ida sat down. Under the cover of her desk she slipped off her shoes. She was aware that if she so much as peeked at Tom, she would burst out laughing again.

"I am sorry to have come at such an awkward moment," Miss Sedgewick began, addressing Ida as well as the class. "I should begin by commending you all for your desire to be in school. As far as *I'm* concerned, there's no harm in your studying together. In fact, I admire it greatly. If you wish to allow Miss Bidson to be your unofficial teacher, there's nothing wrong with that, either."

The other children burst into applause. Ida allowed herself a big smile. The desire to laugh eased.

"However," Miss Sedgewick said with new severity, "as for getting *credit* for what you are doing, that's quite another matter. Credit for the term will require passing an exam given by the county."

Tom raised his hand. "For the eighth graders? Is that what you mean, ma'am?"

"For the eighth graders, certainly. But here's the choice I offer: I'll keep your secret, but in return you must *all* take a final exam."

"All?" Ida said, now very serious.

"All," Miss Sedgewick repeated.

"Me, too?" asked Mary tremulously.

"You, too, my dear."

"I thought tests were just supposed to be for Tom and Ida," Herbert objected.

"Young man, you have changed the rules here," Miss Sedgewick replied. "Now I have, too. You can't get credit for taking a full term unless we see that you have truly mastered it."

"Miss Sedgewick," asked Ida, "can . . . can I see the exams so I can make sure I know what to teach?"

"But then the results would only tell us what you taught your students, Miss Bidson, not what they know. No, my dear, just continue as you've been doing. The test will allow me to see what you have accomplished. Agreed?"

No one spoke.

"Is that a yes or a no?" asked Miss Sedgewick.

"We've been doing everything by voting," Ida said.

"Then please feel free to vote," Miss Sedgewick urged.

Ida stood up. "Those in favor of everybody taking exams like Miss Sedgewick says, raise hands."

All hands—except Herbert's—went up.

"I'm afraid," said Miss Sedgewick, "this won't work unless everyone agrees." She turned to Herbert. "Young man, would you reconsider?"

"Aw,"—he scowled—"if I take that exam, I'm just gonna fail it."

"Herbert, please," Ida pleaded.

Herbert stared down at his desk.

Once more, Ida said, "Those in favor."

This time all hands—including Herbert's—rose.

"Good," said Miss Sedgewick. "Then I shall be here bright and early on the morning of June the seventh to conduct examinations. I presume for you, too, Miss Bidson."

"Yes, ma'am."

"So, if you please, just give me each student's name and grade level."

Ida found a piece of paper, and while the class looked on in silence, she provided the information.

Miss Sedgewick took the paper, folded it up, and placed it in her purse. "I wish each and every one of you good luck," she said, and started for the door. Reaching it, she paused. "Two more things," she said. "I urge you to inform your parents and the school board about what you are doing. And, Miss Bidson, do get into dry clothing before you catch your death of cold."

The children waited until they heard the sound of a car driving away.

"I suppose," said Ida, "we'll just have to work harder."

"And there's one more thing," Herbert called out.

"What's that?"

"No more swimming!"

When Ida and Felix got home that afternoon, Ida went right into the kitchen. Her mother was at the big plank table kneading their weekly bread.

"Ida!" she cried. "What happened to you?"

"We had some fun at school today," Ida said ruefully.

Mrs. Bidson gave her daughter a look. "Ida, are you teaching or playing games down there?"

"I'm *teaching,* Ma," Ida said hotly. Then she told her everything that had happened, including the unfortunate visit by Miss Sedgewick. "Now the whole school has to take exams," Ida said. "I've ruined everything."

"If you had," her mother said, "that woman would have said so."

"In the whole time I've been teaching," Ida said, "it was the only fooling I've done. Anyway, it was fun." She pouted. "The most fun I've had in a long time."

"Ida, a teacher will always be held up as an example to her students."

"That's not fair!" Ida burst out. "I'm a person, too. I should study electricity, like Tom. Or play with a printing press. No one thinks *he's* bad when he's fooling."

"Speaking of bad, I'm afraid I have more unfortunate news," said her mother. "I met Herbert Bixler's pa when your father and I were at the feed store today. He complained to me that Herbert is wasting his time going to school. Said he wants to go to the school board and complain that you're keeping the school open."

"He didn't!"

"Well, perhaps he was just talking big."

"Ma, you know what I think? I think Mr. Bixler doesn't want Herbert to come to school at all!"

"I'm just telling you what he said."

"Or maybe Mr. Bixler's mad at me because I went down to his place," Ida confessed.

"Did you? Why?"

"Ma, it's what teachers do. Herbert hadn't been in school. I'm supposed to find out why. You know what Mr. Bixler said? Said Herbert's schooling doesn't matter."

"Honey, Mr. Bixler's wife died when Herbert was still a baby. Mr. Bixler's had bad luck on his farm. Lost a whole lot of sheep because of disease. Folks say his debt is piling up. He's not a happy man. Unhappy folks do unhappy things."

"Do you think Mr. Jordan already knows what we're doing?"

"Ida, in this valley—sooner or later—everybody knows everything about everybody. You could tell him yourself, you know."

"He'd only say no."

A frowning Ida sat down before the kitchen table.

"Is there something else?" her mother asked.

Ida said nothing.

"Is it Tom?"

Ida shook her head.

"Can't be any worse than what you've already told me, can it?" her mother coaxed.

"Ma...I've been working so hard at teaching, I've been letting my own studying go. Way I'm going, I'll be the only one failing the exam."

"Well, Miss Bidson, however you decide to head off that problem, I suggest you start by getting into some clean clothes."

Thirteen

❦

THAT EVENING AFTER her chores and grading were done, Ida worked late into the night. She began with her reader, focusing on sections she had not read before. She studied grammar and tried to memorize passages, working in particular on "A Psalm of Life," a poem by Longfellow. In the morning she parsed sentences in her head as she milked Bluebell. At the breakfast table she did math problems, her eyes glued to her textbook.

Though her father frowned at her, he said nothing.

As she and Felix drove to school she recited the Longfellow poem:

"Tell me not in mournful numbers—*Brake, clutch!*
Life is but—*Not so hard!*—an empty dream—
For the soul is dead that slumbers—*Brake!*
And things are not—*Brake, clutch!*—what they
    seem.

Life is real!—*Brake!*—Life is earnest!
And the grave—*Clutch!*—is not its goal;
Dust thou art, to dust returnest—*Brake!*
Was not—*Brake! Clutch!*—spoken of the soul.

"We're here!"

In school, right after the morning exercises, Ida stood before the class.

"Anyone know where Herbert is?"

"Working, probably," Charley said.

"I need to know," Ida said, "if our school is still secret. How many of you told your parents what we're doing? I did," she informed them. "Had to."

Tom was the first one to respond. Then, shyly, Natasha raised her hand. Charley said, "I just told ours that school was going on. Didn't say you were teacher."

Ida explained what had happened when she went to Herbert's place and spoke to Mr. Bixler.

"By mistake I told him I was the teacher," she said. "He didn't like it." Then she told them what Mr. Bixler had said to her mother.

"Think he really will say something to Mr. Jordan?" Natasha asked.

"My dad says Mr. Bixler isn't really mean," Susie put in. "Just unhappy all the time."

"My ma said the same," Ida agreed. "I don't know what he'll do. But if you haven't already, I guess you'd better let your parents know everything. Just try to get them not to tell anyone else, specially Mr. Jordan."

She sighed. "Guess we better get on with our own work," Ida said. "Can't be any shirking if we're going to pass those exams."

Ida went to her desk and consulted her notebook, then gave instructions to the class. "Tom, sentence parsing. Mary, penmanship. In particular, your Gs, Qs, and Fs. Susie, I'd like you to help her. Natasha, when you're ready, I'll quiz you on the continents. Charley, reading. Felix, you start off with a recitation of your ABCs."

Everybody set to work.

More than before, Ida put everyone to tasks that they could do on their own. While they set about their assignments, she sat at her desk, secretly working on her own studies—in particular, math. *Secret school. Secret student,* she thought.

Halfway through the morning, Ida walked up to Tom's desk.

"Yes, Miss Bidson," he said.

"Tom," Ida said, whispering so no one else would hear. "I'm not teaching now. I'm studying for myself. How do you do this kind of math problem?"

Tom looked at her, pushed the hair away from his forehead, and gave her a wink.

"Tom," she whispered. *"Please."*

"Okay. Better sit down, though," he said, and showed her how to do the problem.

"Thank you," she whispered, giving him a grateful look when he was done.

In the evening as soon as she got home, Ida raced through her chores, retreated to the loft, and worked on her studies. After dinner she did the same.

Her mother found Ida in bed. By the glowing light of a kerosene lamp she was rereading the school's frayed copy of *Great Orations by Great Men.*

"Ida, it's very late. You're pushing yourself too hard."

"What's the good of me being teacher?" Ida replied with anguish. "If everyone else passes the exams and I don't, it'll be the last time I ever teach."

"Honey, I'm sure you know more than you think."

"Ma, the exam is a couple of weeks away, but I have no idea what's in it. I have to know *everything*."

"Honey, I don't want you getting sick. Won't be good for anything then."

"I'll be a whole lot sicker if I don't get to high school."

Mrs. Bidson sighed and retreated down the ladder.

The next day school started as usual. As the hours passed, it grew darker and darker. Recess was held, but the thunderheads gathering around the mountain peaks made it clear that a big storm was coming.

"We'd best light the lamps and get in some dry wood," Ida said.

Right after lunch the storm struck. It came softly at first, then quickly shifted into roof-rattling hail.

The children gazed around, watching the large hailstones bounce off the windows.

Tom raised his hand.

"Yes, Tom?"

"Can I bring in Ruckus? He gets panicky in hailstorms."

Ida frowned. "You never did when it stormed before."

Tom nodded toward the windows. "That's big hail."

"Very well, I suppose it's all right. But I don't want that mule interfering."

Tom dashed out. Moments later he returned, leading the mule through the schoolhouse door. He looked around, then backed the animal into the boys' wardrobe and shut the door.

With the lamps on and the stove hot, it was cozy in the schoolhouse. The students stayed attentive to their work. Now and again in the wardrobe, the mule stamped and occasionally brayed, but no one paid him any mind.

It was still raining that afternoon when Mary, standing before the class, got ready to recite a poem. The rest of the children were listening intently.

"'The Song of the Bee,'" Mary began.

"This is the song of the bee.

His legs are of yellow,

A jolly, good fellow,

and yet a great worker is he.

In days that are sunny—"

The door burst open. Mr. Jordan stood there, his yellow rain slicker dripping wet. "So it's true what I was told. You *are* meeting here. Well, this school is supposed to be closed. And as of this moment, it *is* closed. Now all of you get on home where you belong!"

No one moved.

Suddenly from the boys' wardrobe, there came a loud stamping.

Puzzled, Mr. Jordan opened the wardrobe door. The mule stuck his head out and brayed in Mr. Jordan's face.

"And get this mule out of here!" Mr. Jordan cried.

Fourteen

❧

THE NEXT DAY Ida and Felix stayed home.
There was no choice.

Felix was more than happy to work along with
his father, helping repair the barns and tend to the
sheep in the fields. Ida, however, woke that morning completely miserable. No teaching. No exams.
No high school. No future. She was trapped. And
it was her own fault. If only she hadn't spoken to
Herbert's father!

Though she wanted to, she knew she couldn't
lay abed doing nothing. She did her regular chores
before breakfast, then took care of the baby when

her mother asked her to. The spring sheepshearing had begun.

Ida took Shelby up to the loft and tried to entertain him with one of her schoolbooks.

"I could teach you your ABCs," she offered. The little boy studied her with large, uncomprehending eyes.

"'*A* is for apple pie,'" Ida began, pointing to the letter in the book. Shelby, however, suddenly reached forward and grabbed hold of a page. Ida just managed to keep him from tearing it.

"All right," she said with a sigh. "Let's go for a walk."

She took the boy's hand and they made their way, with Shelby waddling, from their log house to the stream back behind it. Still hoping to do some reading, Ida brought along her book.

At the water's edge, Shelby squatted and placed his hands, palms down, into the water—still cold and high from mountain snow runoff—and laughed. Ida, for safety's sake, sat close behind him, watching. She wondered what Tom was doing. Probably, she thought with a pang of envy, printing church circulars or fiddling with his radio, listening to the world. She picked up her book but didn't open it.

"Shelby," Ida said, "what am I going to do?"

Shelby slapped the water with his hands, making a splash that wet him. First startled, he then laughed with delight and did it again.

"Slapping the water won't help *me*," Ida said with a sigh. Leaning back against a tree, she opened her book and tried to read. Every so often she glanced up to make sure the boy was safe. The result was she read only by bits and pieces, hardly taking in any meaning. The way she was feeling, the words before her seemed empty.

She was only staring at the book when she suddenly felt a poke on her left shoulder. Startled, she turned. No one was there. She turned back to her book. Standing in front of her was a grinning Herbert.

"Fooled you!" he cried.

"How'd you get here?" she asked.

"Walked," he said. "Hey, you Ida or Miss Bidson now?" he asked.

"Guess I'm nothing but Ida," she replied glumly. "What are you doing here?"

"Nothing," he said. "Just thought I'd come by and say howdy."

"Herbert Bixler," she replied, "don't tell me you walked seven miles just to say hello."

Herbert grinned again. "Maybe I did. Maybe I didn't. That your baby brother?" he asked.

"That's Shelby all right."

"See you got a book. Trying to teach him now?"

"Can't use the school, can I?" Ida said, suddenly feeling cross. "Which probably makes you happy."

"How so?"

"You don't like school."

Herbert looked at his feet. Wiggled his toes. "Hey," he said, "no kid is gonna say they *like* school. 'Cause if they do, other kids will rag on him."

"But you don't like it," Ida said accusingly.

Herbert still didn't look up. "Come on, Ida. There's lots of work on my dad's place," he said. "Just him and me, you know."

"I know," Ida said, already sorry she had spoken so sharply.

Herbert was quiet for a moment. Then, without looking at Ida directly, he said, "See, my dad, he never had much learning. Sometimes I think he gets fretted up about me knowing more than he does. Worries I'll get uppity. Thinks if I know too much, I might take off. You know, hightail it somewhere far away. Never come back. Which I just might do. Someday. Angry old cuss, he is. Lonely, too."

"Is that why he told Mr. Jordan about our school?"

Herbert looked around. There was no grin on his face now. "Guess he did. Wasn't me who told Dad about it, though. Knew he'd object. You told him. He was pretty sore. Called me a liar. Then, couple of days ago, he told me how stupid I was. I got so mad, I let him know something about my learning."

"How did you do that?"

Herbert grinned. "I just stood there, pitching hay, and recited that whole darn speech from Shake-speare. You know, that one in the reader from *Julius Caesar*? The one Tom couldn't understand? 'Friends, Romans, countrymen, lend me your ears; I come to bury Caesar, not to praise him.'"

Ida, feeling her anger melt, laughed and clapped her hands. "I didn't know you knew that speech," she said.

"How many years have I been going to that school? And how many kids had to learn that speech? I guess I heard it enough, didn't I?

"Anyway," Herbert went on, "I was going on like that, mighty high and powerful. Pretty soon the old man got so mad, he just took off. Guess that's when he told Jordan what we were doing. I think he wanted to fix it so I couldn't learn any more speeches."

Ida studied him. "Herbert Bixler, can I tell you something?"

"Sure."

"You are really smart. How come you won't act it?"

"'Cause I'm dumb."

Ida sighed. "How'd you know I was down here?" she asked. "My ma tell you?"

"Nope. She don't know I'm here. I just watched till you showed. Followed you here. Don't mind, do you?"

"No," she said. "And you can sit. You've walked a long way."

"Don't mind if I do."

Shelby splashed and laughed.

They watched him for a while. "Wish I were like that," Herbert said.

"Why?"

"I suppose he don't know much of anything. I tell you, Miss Bidson, knowing things can worry you deep."

"I never saw you worried."

"Maybe not before."

Ida considered him anew. Herbert looked very

serious. "But if you did worry," she asked carefully, "what kind of things would you be worried about now?"

"Well," Herbert drawled, "suppose a fellow knew there was going to be a school board meeting? And suppose that meeting was to make sure school stayed shut? And suppose that meeting was going to be held, not exactly secret, you see, but real quiet so people wouldn't know—except for folks like my dad who don't like schools much? And suppose, even, my dad bragged to me how there wouldn't *be* any school for me to go to anymore, 'cause, see, no one who likes schooling would be able to show up at that meeting because they wouldn't know about it?"

Ida's heart started hammering. "Herbert, when's a body to suppose that meeting would take place?"

"I guess he'd suppose it'd be tomorrow evening, seven sharp. At the schoolhouse. That's what."

"Herbert Bixler, is that what *you* suppose?"

"I do, Miss Bidson," Herbert returned with a grin. "I surely do."

"And what would you do about it?"

"I don't exactly know, but if I was you, I'd do *something*. Make sure the right people show up."

"Herbert Bixler," said Ida, smiling, "I do like you. I truly do."

Not looking at her, Herbert poked at his feet. "Better than Tom?"

Ida blushed, scooped up some water, and flung it at him. "Shooo!" she cried.

Herbert laughed, jumped up, and ran away.

Momentarily Ida looked after him, then grabbed Shelby's hand. "Come on. We got a whole lot of work to do."

Fifteen

✑

"MA, PA!" IDA CRIED, as she rushed into the barn, Shelby in her arms. "Mr. Jordan's called a school board meeting for tomorrow evening without telling people. It's to make sure the school stays shut down."

"Now hold on," her father said, "if he didn't tell, how'd you know?" He and Mrs. Bidson were shearing sheep. Mrs. Bidson was holding them steady while Mr. Bidson did the clipping.

Breathless, Ida explained about Herbert's visit and what he had said.

"That doesn't seem very fair," Mrs. Bidson said when Ida had finished.

"I have to tell everyone that it's happening," Ida said. "Get people to come to the meeting. And it's tomorrow night. Oh, why can't we have a telephone like they do in town?"

"Honey, there's not one soul in the valley that has a telephone."

Mr. and Mrs. Bidson released the sheep they had been shearing. For a moment he just stood there as if not sure what had happened to him. Then, with a shake of his head and a bleat, he bolted off.

"Can I take the car and go now? With Felix?"

"Ida, there's so much going on right—"

"Please," Ida cried, her eyes filling with tears. "This is the most important thing in my whole life! This summer, after school, all day, all the time, I'll work double hard. Triple hard. I'll take care of—"

"Ida," her mother interrupted sharply, "your pa's not trying to drive a bargain. You can see what's going on. You're needed here."

"I'm sorry," Ida managed, gazing at her parents, her tears streaming. "Please, *please*," she implored, "I have to tell people about the meeting. I have to. Can I go, *please*?"

Mr. and Mrs. Bidson exchanged looks. Finally Mrs. Bidson said, "Course you can."

"And don't you worry," Mr. Bidson added. "We'll get to the meeting, too. When did you say it was?"

"Tomorrow night," Ida said, thrusting the baby into her mother's arms, then flying out of the barn. "Felix! I need you! Felix!"

Felix was behind the house, stacking small logs for the kitchen stove. She grabbed his hand and raced for the car.

"What's the matter?" Felix asked as they drove down the long driveway.

Ida explained as best she could. "And we have to tell everyone in the valley," she concluded.

"Maybe Tom could put it on his radio," Felix suggested.

"I don't think it works that way," she said. Then, in a burst of inspiration, she cried, "But he could print us up a circular. Come on! Clutch and gas!"

"Ah, ja, it's Ida and Felix Bidson," Tom's mother said, greeting the two of them at the porch door, apron around her waist, hands white with flour. She was a short, heavyset woman, with plump red cheeks. "Not seen you for the age of the dog. Though, you know, I hear all about you,

Ida, from our own Tom. You two come right on in. My pleasure. And your mother, she is good?"

"They're fine. Mrs. Kohl, I'm looking for Tom. I have to speak to him right away."

"Sure you do. Miss Ida, Tom says you are always doing fine things at the school. Being the good teacher, he says."

"Mrs. Kohl," Ida said, unable to contain her excitement, "something important is happening." She told the woman about the meeting.

"For shame! That's Mr. Jordan himself. Always thinking he's in charge of the whole world. A regular Kaiser. Ja, we had better be there, too."

"Can I speak to Tom?"

"You can, ja. He's over to the barn with his father. You know where that is, I think."

"Thank you, Mrs. Kohl."

"Go right on now. Mr. Felix, you find Mary and then come to the kitchen for a something. Miss Ida, say the hello to your mother."

Ida flew out of the house, across the yards, and into the Kohls' barn. It was a large structure, sweet with the smell of stacked hay.

Tom was on his back, under a truck that he and his father were repairing. Mr. Kohl was kneeling by his side, handing in tools.

"Who's that there?" he demanded as Ida approached. Mr. Kohl was a large man, with big features and a loud voice rich with a German accent, like his wife's.

"It's me, Mr. Kohl. Ida Bidson."

"Oh, I see you now, Ida. For sure that's you. How do you do? Tom," he said, giving a poke to his son, "here comes a visitor for you, I think. Not me."

Tom pushed himself out from beneath the truck and looked up.

"Hi!" he called.

"Tom," Ida said, too excited to make small talk, "Mr. Jordan's holding a secret school-board meeting tomorrow. To make sure the school stays closed. We have to get people there. You need to print up a circular."

"What's all this, now?" Mr. Kohl asked.

Ida explained how Herbert had come and what he had said. "Tom, if you could print up something, and we could spread it around so people in the valley would come, it might help."

"I guess I could," Tom said. "But...Ida, I got this to do..." He looked to his father.

"No, no," said Mr. Kohl. "That's all right. I understand. You've got yourself a good idea, Ida. The missus and I will go to the meeting, too. For sure. Tom, you do like Ida said. I'll finish here myself."

Tom and Ida headed back toward the house. Tom asked, "What's the circular to say?"

"I hadn't thought of that," Ida admitted. She considered for a moment. "Maybe, 'School meeting: Is school to be open or closed? Wednesday, seven o'clock.' Could you do all that?"

Tom thought for a moment, counting on his fingers.

"What are you counting?"

"Os. Remember, I don't have a whole lot of them."

"Can we try, anyway?"

"Sure."

One hour later they pulled the first circular from the press.

Meeting at School!!!
School `pen 0r cl-sed?
Wed. 7 pm

Tom handed it to Ida. "Think it'll do?"

"It'll have to."

They printed off twenty sheets, then agreed who would go where, Tom on Ruckus, and Ida and Felix in the car to places farther away.

"Oh, Tom, do you think people will come?" Ida asked as she opened the car door for Felix.

"Don't know," he said. "Worth trying, though. And at the meeting, you're going to have to say something."

"Me? Why?"

"The teacher always talks at board meetings. And—in case you forgot—you're the teacher."

Sixteen

❦

THE NEXT EVENING the meeting of the Elk
Valley School Board began on time. Mr. Jordan
was there. So was Mr. Hawkins, the Methodist
minister, a roly-poly man, too large for the dark
suit he wore, and Mr. Morris, a down-valley sheep
rancher, dressed in his working clothes. By his side
was Mr. Plumstead, looking very formal in his suit
with high white collar, tie, and wire-frame eye-
glasses. The four sat on a bench brought forward
for the occasion.

All eight schoolchildren, including Herbert,
sat in a row before the board. They had gotten
there early. Their parents sat behind them. Though

Herbert was there, his father wasn't. But some dozen other men and women from the valley were in the back of the room. When Mr. Jordan had arrived, he had been surprised to see so many people.

"Seems to me," Mr. Jordan opened the meeting by saying, "we've got ourselves quite a mess here. This school was supposed to be closed. But not only was it kept open, Ida Bidson was pretending to be the teacher."

"And I'm afraid," interjected Mr. Plumstead, "I saw Miss Fletcher lock the front door. She gave me the key and I gave the key to you, Mr. Jordan. In other words, these children have been trespassing on township property. How did you get in?"

"Through the window," Herbert blurted out.

One of the parents in the audience barely suppressed a laugh.

"But may I ask," interrupted Mr. Hawkins, the minister, "if there's been any damage done to the building? You inspected it, Mr. Jordan. Any problems?"

Mr. Jordan pointed to the boys' wardrobe. "When I came in the other day, a mule was in there."

That time the crowd broke into laughter.

"Did you do an inspection?" Mr. Hawkins persisted.

"Well, yes. There was no damage," Mr. Jordan admitted. "But trespassing is trespassing. And a mule doesn't belong in school."

"Oh, I don't know," Mr. Morris drawled. "I can remember a few two-legged ones from my days."

The audience laughed again.

"Now, sir," said Mr. Hawkins, "I can't speak about mules, but seems to me these children were just trying to get on with their education. Fact is, gentlemen, I didn't even know Miss Fletcher was gone. Leastwise, Mr. Jordan, you never informed me. Did you know?" he asked Mr. Morris.

"Only recently."

"Too late to get a replacement," Mr. Jordan growled. "Didn't want to bother you."

"I accept your explanation, sir," said Mr. Hawkins. "But I can't see how these children did any real harm. Fact, I'd say they were only doing what we want them to do—learn. And I say, more power to them."

The audience applauded.

Looking uncomfortable, Mr. Jordan said, "But this girl"—he pointed to Ida—"this Ida Bidson was *pretending* to be a teacher. Can't pay the girl if she's got no license."

"*Did* you pay her?" called someone from the audience.

"Course not," Mr. Jordan said. "She isn't licensed."

"Then, sir, she saved us a considerable sum of money, didn't she?" said Mr. Hawkins.

Once again the room erupted with laughter.

Ida raised her hand.

"What do you want?" Mr. Jordan demanded.

"May I say something, please?" she said.

"I don't know as how—"

"Oh, let the girl speak, sir," Mr. Morris suggested. "After all, you have accused her of wrongdoing."

The other men on the board nodded.

Ida rose up from her bench seat. "Mr. Jordan, we didn't mean any harm. It's just that both Tom and I want to go on to high school so badly. Tom's going to be an electric specialist. I want to be a teacher. But we need to finish our schooling for that. And we need to take the exit exam so we can go. The other children wanted to move on, too, and not repeat anything. We did everything by votes. Majority always ruled."

"You can say that again," Herbert cried out.

"In conclusion," Ida went on, "I should like to recite a poem Miss Fletcher taught us."

"We don't do poetry at school board meetings," Mr. Jordan said gruffly.

"Might be a noble thing if we did," Mr. Hawkins said.

Red faced, Mr. Jordan said, "Well, I suppose you can do your piece."

Ida, hands extended, and gesturing dramatically as she spoke, began:

> "Do what conscience says is right;
> Do what reason says is best;
> Do with all your mind and might;
> Do your duty, and be blest."

Ida paused, then said, "Please, sirs, the term is almost over. Miss Sedgewick from the County Education Office said she'd come and test us all. We'd just appreciate it if you gave us the chance to try."

There was great applause from the crowd, even some stamping of feet.

As Ida sat down, Tom whispered, "Pretty corny but a great old job!"

The members of the school board excused themselves and went out to the porch. While they were conferring, everyone else grouped around Ida, congratulating her.

Finally, the four men trooped back in and sat down.

"We've had our discussion," a grim-looking Mr. Jordan began. "We're going to let this . . . secret school go forward for two more weeks with Ida Bidson as the teacher, so the children can take their exams. But that's the only reason."

There were cheers from the audience.

A beaming Ida stood up. "Thank—"

Mr. Jordan held up a hand. "Hold on. Hold on! There are some conditions. First, the families whose children are involved must take responsibility for the school building and grounds. Second, we expect every child to pass their exams. If they don't, I want the whole valley to know—it won't be the board's doing, it'll be the teacher's!"

With that Mr. Jordan promptly stood up and marched out of the room. The other board members mingled with the excited crowd.

Ida sat still for a moment, and then allowed herself an enormous sigh of relief.

"Guess you did it again," Tom said.

Ida looked at her hands. "Thank you."

"I guess you are one airtight girl."

Startled, Ida looked around. "What's that supposed to mean?"

Tom grinned. "You know . . . swell."

"Where'd you get those words?"

He shrugged. "On the radio."

Impulsively, Ida gave him a hug. Then she felt a rush of confusion, blushed deeply, and ran outside. The night sky, cloudless and moonless, was blossoming with a million stars. There seemed no end to them. *We won,* Ida exalted. *We won!*

Then she checked herself. *No, not yet. I must pass the exam.*

Seventeen

ↂ

THE LAST TWO WEEKS of school were frantic. The students spent every day quizzing one another, going over recitations, parsing sentences, working on penmanship. Though Ida announced morning and afternoon recess, no one—except Herbert—took either. When lunchtime came, everyone ate inside.

For Ida it was a time of torment. She felt like yelling, "Let *me* study! It's *my* turn!" But her students—the younger ones in particular—kept asking for help. How could she refuse? She was the teacher. Hadn't Mr. Jordan said she was responsible?

The day before the exams, Ida's head ached painfully from trying to remember everything. She could only assume everyone else was feeling the same.

"Be on time! Be on time!" they called to one another as they went their separate ways after school.

"Herbert?" Ida asked. "You going to be here tomorrow?"

The boy grinned. "May be or may *not* be," he said, walking backward away from her.

"Herbert," she said fiercely, "I want you to pass."

He stopped. "You do?"

"I want you to show everyone how smart you are."

For just a moment Herbert's face turned sad. Then he grinned, winked, and turned away, saying, "Never know with me!"

Tom walked up to the front of the old Ford. "Want to study together?" he asked.

"I think I'd do better at home," Ida said quickly. Seeing the flash of hurt on his face, she added, "Tom, I have to concentrate, and I just can't do it if I'm not alone."

She fairly raced the Model T home.

That night Ida worked late into the evening, reading and rereading, trying to remember and review the whole year's work. When Felix came to her with his primer and asked for help, she begged him to go to one of their parents. When he did, she felt so guilty she went to help him, got frustrated, then came back to her own work.

Before she went to bed, she made her father promise to get her up earlier than usual. Then she read herself into fitful sleep.

It was the day of the exam.

Ida didn't need to be woken. She was already half awake at four o'clock. She read some more, then raced quickly to the barn.

It was raining, and the yards were muddy. In her haste, Ida slipped twice, banging her knees hard and muddying her clothing.

"I can't do it," Ida said to herself as she milked Bluebell. "I had to help everybody pass their exams. They mustn't, *mustn't* fail. It's going to be my fault if they do. *I'm* responsible. I was the teacher."

Ida had resisted tears for so long, but now, exhausted and wrought up, she finally let them come. The deep, racking sobs were loud enough to cause the cow to turn around and see what was happening.

Ashamed, Ida pushed her face against Bluebell's belly, dried her tears with the hem of her nightgown, then finished the milking. Composing herself, she carefully brought the full bucket into the kitchen.

"What's the matter, Ida?" her mother asked.

Ida shook her head. "Nothing," she said.

Mrs. Bidson continued to stare at her. "Yes, there is," she persisted. "You've been crying."

"Ma, I'm so tired!"

"Look at me."

"Don't want to."

"Honey, I need to tell you something. Your pa and I are really proud of you. You've worked very hard."

"Ma, I keep remembering what Mr. Jordan said: Girls don't need to go to high school."

"Only shows that some grown-ups could use some schooling themselves."

Ida smiled and gave her mother a quick hug, then climbed into the loft, and changed her clothes. She started to put up her hair—as she had been doing every morning since she'd begun teaching—then remembered she didn't need to anymore. "I'm a student again," she muttered.

"Come on, get dressed," she told Felix as she woke him. "Can't be late for exam day. It's raining. Wear your slicker. The road's going to be bad."

They left a little early, Felix taking his place among the pedals and Ida clutching the steering wheel with two hands.

Both their parents waved them off, calling, "Good luck!"

As Ida and Felix drove along, the rain was still coming down hard, making it difficult to see. The windowless doors meant they were getting wet, too. Besides, Ida's head was so full of facts and figures, she had a hard time concentrating on the road.

"Ida," Felix called up when they were about halfway along their journey, "what's the matter?"

"Nothing."

"You think we're going to fail, don't you?"

"You're going to do fine."

"Then what?"

"Felix," Ida snapped, "I'm trying to think about my own test." She wiped the rainwater off her face.

"Do you think you'll fail?"

"Stop talking to me!" Ida yelled at him, and pulled down the gas lever. The car accelerated faster than Ida expected. "Brake! Brake!" she yelled.

Frightened by the alarm in Ida's voice, Felix shoved down the brake pedal with both hands.

The wheels locked. The car skidded. Ida spun the wheel. Too late. The car slid into a ditch. The motor backfired and died.

"What happened?" Felix asked.

"We've gone off the road," Ida said, horrified.

Ida sat there, leaning on the wheel, too numb to do anything.

Felix crawled up to the seat next to her. "Ida," he asked cautiously as he tried to peer outside, "how far are we from school?"

"I don't know," Ida said. "Halfway, maybe."

"What are we going to do?"

"Walk, I suppose."

"We . . . going to miss the exams?"

Ida said nothing.

"*Are* we?"

"Probably."

"But we have do something!" Felix cried.

Ida peered out through the windshield. It was so spattered with leaves and mud that she couldn't see anything.

Suddenly a face appeared at the side door. Felix and Ida jumped. Tom, his hair plastered down with rain, was standing there. Mary was by his side.

"What you doing?" Tom asked, grinning. "Playing hooky?"

Ida didn't know whether to laugh or cry.

"Want a lift?" Tom said. "I'm pretty sure old Ruckus can carry us all."

They were the last ones to get to school, but Miss Sedgewick had not yet arrived. The rain had probably delayed her, too.

Ida looked around. Natasha had lit the lamps. Herbert had started the fire. The room was neat save for a few muddy footprints on the floor.

"Thank you, everyone. Let's take our seats."

Ida went to the teacher's desk and made sure that sharp pencils were ready and that the blackboard was clean and supplied with chalk.

There was a knock on the door. Felix ran to open it. It was Miss Sedgewick. This time, aside from her purse, she carried a briefcase and an umbrella. "May I come in, Miss Bidson?" she asked.

"Yes, please. And I'm just Ida today."

Miss Sedgewick looked at Ida's wet hair and

smiled. "Have you been swimming again?" she asked.

"The rain," Ida said lamely. "My car ran off the road. Tom and Mary had to rescue us."

"Oh dear!" said Miss Sedgewick. "Can you take your exam?"

"I want to," Felix said.

"Me, too," said Ida.

Miss Sedgewick smiled broadly then said, "Then we had best begin. Tom—that is your name?"

"Yes, ma'am."

"As the day progresses, I'd like you to keep the fire going."

Ida went to her old place on the bench next to Tom. He gave her an encouraging smile. Feeling very tense, Ida tried to smile back but barely succeeded.

Miss Sedgewick opened her briefcase. "There are two parts to your exams," she announced to the students. "There are written sections"—she held up some little booklets—"and there are recitations and board exercises. When I call your name, please close your test booklets completely and come forward to the desk for these exercises. I'll start with the youngest and work my way up.

"I see your teacher, Miss Bidson, has some pencils ready for you. Excellent. Now, children, I've put each of your names on the cover of the proper test booklet. Please look to make sure you have your own," she said as she passed them out.

When everything was ready she took a hand-bell from her bag. "When I ring this, begin. When I ring it again, we'll take rests, recess, and so forth. Now"—she rang the bell—"begin."

The children opened their booklets. Natasha and Tom immediately began to write.

Taking a deep breath, Ida quickly leafed through her booklet. The table of contents listed exams in writing, reading, spelling, grammar, arithmetic, geography, U.S. history, and science.

Ida then opened the book at random and came upon geography. The first question was:

Compare South America to North America in terms of size, shape, principal products, and population.

Ida's stomach lurched.

Miss Sedgewick called, "Felix Bidson! Please come forward and let me hear your ABCs."

Nervously Ida turned to arithmetic. The first question was:

A farmer hired a man and a boy at a yearly expense of $480. The man received $25 a month. What part of the $480 did the boy receive?

Ida groaned inwardly and then looked around the room. By the teacher's desk, Felix was reciting the alphabet in a loud singsong. Everyone else was bent over their tests. Ida could hear the soft scratching of pencils, the rub of erasers. Her damp hair made her scalp itch.

Panic gripped her. She was wasting precious time! *You have to pass,* she scolded herself. *You must! Start!* Picking up a pencil, she turned to the front page of the test booklet.

READING

Choose a poem you have learned this year from your reader. Provide the title, the author, the dates of his or her birth, and if such is the case, his or her death. Write out all the stanzas of the poem. Then write a brief essay as to why the poem is important to you.

I can do that, Ida thought with enormous relief, and began to write.

The day seemed to race by. Even though the rain had stopped by morning recess, no one wanted to be out for long other than to stretch and drink a cup of water. Lunch was much the same. Food was bolted, not eaten. After lunch Mary and Felix went to play outside because their tests were finished.

The others continued.

At two-thirty in the afternoon, Miss Sedgewick rang the handbell. "Half an hour," she informed them. "Check your work."

Then, "Five minutes! Make sure your name is on everything."

Finally the last bell. "Please write your post box number under your name on your booklet's front cover," she instructed.

That done, Miss Sedgewick collected the booklets and packed them away.

"How will we know if we passed?" Ida asked her.

"I shall start grading them tomorrow. When I have finished them all, you'll be informed by mail." She offered an encouraging smile and left.

Ida went up to the teacher's desk. Everyone was looking at her. In all her life she had never felt so drained. "I guess that's it," she said. "Thank you for working so hard. I'm sure everyone passed."

The children, too tired to say anything, filed outside.

After everyone else left, Ida remained, looking over the empty schoolroom. It seemed strange without students. She wasn't sure what she felt most, sad or weary.

Taking up her father's clock and sheepskin from the desk drawer, as well as her lunch pail from the girls' wardrobe, Ida walked outside.

Tom was waiting, along with Mary and Felix.

"How'd you do?" Tom asked Ida as she closed the door behind her.

"I don't know," she confessed. Then she looked more carefully at the three of them. They seemed very somber. "Is something the matter?" she asked.

Tom grinned. "Thought maybe you'd want us to help pull your car out of the mud."

Eighteen

THE WEEK FOLLOWING THE exam was a nerve-racking time for Ida.

She found staying at home extremely difficult. But at least there were always things that had to be done.

The worst part was worrying over the exam results. Ida could barely wait for the end of each day. Then she and Felix would drive about a mile down the road to check their battered mailbox, one of a line of seven for those families living at the head of Elk Valley.

For six days, when Ida and Felix arrived, the

red mailbox flag was down. Then, exactly one week after the day of the exam, the flag was up.

"They're here!" Ida screamed at Felix as they drew close. "Clutch. Brake!"

The car skittered and backfired to a stop. Not waiting for Felix, Ida untied the door, leaped out, and raced to the box.

Inside were two pale tan envelopes, each one addressed in an elegant scrolling hand. One was for "Miss Ida Bidson," the other for "Master Felix Bidson."

Handing Felix his envelope, Ida tore open her own. Inside was a printed form with parts filled in by hand:

> *This certifies that <u>Ida Bidson</u>, age <u>14</u>, a resident of the town of <u>Elk Valley</u>, of <u>Routt</u> County, State of Colorado, has completed the course of study <u>with honors</u> prescribed for common schools, and is entitled to enter the high school at <u>Steamboat Springs</u>, for the year beginning <u>September 1925</u>.*

> *Yours truly,*
> *Miss Gertrude Sedgewick*
> *County Examiner*

There was yet a second piece of paper, with another note.

Dear Miss Bidson,

I'm happy to inform you that all of your students—except Herbert Bixler—completed their exams with varying degrees of success. Congratulations!

Gertrude Sedgewick
County Examiner

"I passed!" Ida screamed. "Most everyone passed!"

"Did I?" asked Felix as he studied his paper intently.

"You sure did," Ida assured him.

"Did Herbert?"

Ida shook her head.

"How come?"

"I don't think he wanted to," Ida said. She looked at her papers again.

Only then did she notice there was yet a third piece of paper in the envelope, on which a note was written.

My dear Ida,

I have been most impressed by you and what you have done these past weeks. If you would care to take board in my Steamboat Springs home when you attend high school in the fall, I would be happy to have you. It would cost your parents nothing. You may consider it a scholarship.

C. S.

"Felix," Ida said breathlessly.

"What?"

"I think I'm going to high school."

Last Day Exercises were held a week later in the one-room schoolhouse. The students had bedecked it with flowers.

The ceremonies, over which Mr. Jordan presided, began outside with the raising of the flag. Then everyone trooped inside. At the last moment even Herbert appeared, without shoes but with a grin.

One by one the students—youngest to oldest—went to the front of the room to recite. There were poems, excerpts from famous orations, speeches from Shakespeare (to Ida's delight, Herbert recited his *Caesar* speech), and other bits and pieces from literature, all from their readers.

Interspersed were songs sung by all the children. Finally, each student (except Herbert) was handed a certificate of promotion, then given a handshake from the members of the school board.

Ida was the last one to be called.

As she stepped up to receive her diploma, Mr. Jordan cleared his throat. "In addition to graduating from eighth grade with honors," he said, "Miss Ida Bidson, who acted as our schoolteacher, deserves special recognition. I guess"—he cleared his throat—"we can *all* see that."

The adults applauded. The children cheered.

"And here's hoping," Mr. Jordan continued, "she'll go on and become a real teacher, then come on back to work here at this same school."

Herbert shouted out, "But you'll have to pay her then!"

After the laughter died down, Susie—in new shoes and a new dress made just for the occasion—concluded the ceremony by singing "Amazing Grace."

Then everyone headed outside for refreshments. A trestle table had been set up, and people had brought enough food and lemonade to feed the whole valley.

After filling her plate, Ida noticed Herbert standing alone, away from the crowd. She went up to him.

"Well, it's Miss Bidson," he said.

"Herbert Bixler, did you fail that exam on purpose?" she asked.

"Hey, I told you, I'm dumb."

"You are not. You just didn't want to get your father mad, did you?"

Herbert shrugged. "If you want to know, I've made up my mind what I'm going to do."

"What's that?"

"When I get to be old enough, I'm going on down to Denver to join the navy."

"The navy?"

"Sail the seven seas."

"Did you tell your father?"

"Nope. You're the only one who knows."

"And I guess you figure never to come back."

"I dunno. Maybe I will. Depends who's around."

"Herbert Bixler," said Ida, "this may have been a secret school, but you're the biggest secret of all."

Herbert looked at her. She wished she knew what he was thinking. But then he turned and walked away.

She was still looking after him when Tom sidled up. "Hey, Miss Bidson," he said, "thanks for being our teacher."

"You're welcome," Ida managed to say. "Thanks for the idea in the first place."

"Yeah, but now that it's all over, do you know what I like most about it?"

"No."

"I can call you Ida again. All the time."

"I'd like that."

"Hey, Ida," he said with a grin, "want some lemonade?"

"Do you, Tom?"

"Sure as aces."

"We're real proud of you, Ida," her mother said as the family drove home.

"Real proud," Mr. Bidson agreed. "Only thing is, you've got some serious work cut out for you this summer."

"Why?" Ida said, slightly alarmed.

"Well, you'll be going to high school in the fall, right? Boarding with Miss Sedgewick. That means we'll be losing a strong pair of hands. The more work you get done this summer, the easier it's going to be for the rest of us when you go."

"Get Tom up here!" Felix shouted. "He'll do anything for Ida."

Mr. and Mrs. Bidson laughed. Ida's face turned red. But she smiled and looked out the window, and though it was dark outside, all she could see was brightness.

OAKLAND MEDIA CENTER